Archive Fevers

Beyond Criticism Editions explores the new paths that criticism might take in the 21st century.

We encourage any kind of formal adventure: analytical, aphoristic, archival, autobiographical, citational, confessional, descriptive, dialogical, dramatic, fantastical, fictive, graphic, historical, imaginative, ironical, metaphysical, miscellaneous, mythical, palimpsestic, parasitical, philosophical, poetical, polemical, political, probational, riddling, theological, theoretical, ventriloquial.

Our only criterion is that it *discovers*.

The series is curated by Katharine Craik (Oxford Brookes University) and Simon Palfrey (Oxford University)

Archive Fevers

by Tara Blake

BOILER HOUSE PRESS
Beyond Criticism Editions

For Janet

ACKNOWLEDGMENTS

This book could not have been written without the expertise and diligence of archivists at the Screen Archive South East and Library of Congress. The research at these two archives was fully funded by a grant from the Arts and Humanities Research Council in conjunction with a Fellowship at the Kluge Center at the Library of Congress. The writing of the research into a book was aided through a residency at the Hosking Houses Trust. I am very grateful to these organizations for their practical and financial support of this project.

For their unwavering encouragement and reading of various drafts of the manuscript I'd like to thank my wife and muse, Janet, friends Ellen, Judith and Rosa, and late mother, Gay. Gratitude is also due to my children; my daughter for her boundless enthusiasm for grown-up books she can't yet read and my son for his quiet incisiveness.

Contents

Prologue (2021) — **5**

Part I: DC Emails (1997) — **11**

Part II: Unread Emails (1998-2009) — **73**

Part III: Posthumous Emails (2021 & 2010) — **161**

Epilogue (2021) — **223**

Monologue with Derrida (2011) — **229**

Above all, and this is the most serious. . . . [T]here is no archive fever without the threat of this death drive, this aggression and destructive drive.

Jacques Derrida, *Archive Fever* (1995)

Prologue
January 2021

It arrived several whiskeys into a wet winter night during the depths of the COVID pandemic. The automated email, which under normal circumstances I would have been too busy to open, informed me that if I did not act now, my Hotmail account would become unrecoverable due to inactivity. I barely remembered setting up the account and had not used it this side of the year 2000, but I did not like the idea of it becoming 'unrecoverable', of my messages being obliterated or sealed within a digital grave; wherever, or whatever, that is. So, I clicked on the 'recovery' link and took the steps required of me to reactivate my account.

Unsure of what to do when confronted with an inbox unopened for more than twenty years, I navigated the pages of spam by clicking on the button that re-ordered the messages from oldest to newest rather than newest to oldest, as they would usually be displayed. The reverse-ordered pages were filled with messages from a woman whose name seemed familiar but about whom I could not immediately recall any details. The first message from Scarlett Durand arrived in June 1997 and several pages of opened messages from her followed, to which I had replied, until August 1997 when the messages seemed to stop. On re-reading a little of the correspondence, I recalled that Scarlett had been a patient of mine in the mid 1990s who, a year or so into the therapy, had moved from London to Washington DC for several months to pursue a research project in the archives of the Library of Congress.

Scarlett, a junior academic in her late twenties, could be shrewd and forceful but also uncertain and fearful. She said she was unsure whether her thoughts and feelings were truly her own, whether they came from within or without. In sessions with her I sometimes had the sinking sense that I had done something very wrong, that I might have horribly intruded into Scarlett, violating her sense of self. At others, I felt controlled, almost dominated, by her; as though she had got into me, and I had to work very hard to maintain my position as her therapist.

What remains most vividly in my mind about Scarlett is an exchange between us which began with her comment that my consulting room was 'like a vampire's lair'. Admittedly, she was not the first nor the last of my patients to make a comment along these lines about my consulting room which, with its gothic furniture, red carpets and rich, velvet curtains blocking all but the smallest amount of light, did frequently provoke vampiric fantasies. However, what followed was unusual. Reading Scarlett's comment as a fear of me, the therapist, intruding into and depleting her, I responded, 'As if I'm a vampire who might bite you and suck your blood?' to which she immediately retorted, 'No, as if the light outside would kill you.' It was from this association that I began to understand something important about Scarlett's internal world; the fragility of her maternal object, and her fear of her own destructiveness, a destructiveness more potent than I first realised.

Back in 1997, I was a newly qualified therapist in my forties and, like the majority of my colleagues, would not have considered replacing in-person psychotherapy sessions with phone or video consultations. This is ironic given that under the present pandemic conditions I see all my patients either by phone or video. Usually, if a patient were to be out of the country, they would simply have missed their sessions (or, earlier in the twentieth century, they might have received help via letter) but, as the therapy with Scarlett was well-established, and her mother had recently been diagnosed with cancer, I felt it would be best that we maintained a therapeutic relationship of sorts while she spent most of the year abroad, assuming we would resume regular sessions in my consulting room when she returned to London. So, I suggested that, in the place of her weekly fifty-minute in-person sessions, we used the newly developed technology of 'electronic mail' or 'E-mail', as it was written then, to continue the treatment. I asked Scarlett to write for approximately fifty minutes each week, at our regular session time, noting whatever came to her mind in the moment, and email it to me. She agreed to this and I created the Hotmail account to receive her messages. I let her know that I would read the emails and respond each week but that my replies would be brief, for reasons of confidentiality and boundaries.

This experiment in e-therapy did not end well: The therapeutic relationship we had developed during our in-person sessions deteriorated and I found I could not connect with Scarlett via email as I did in the room. Scarlett decided to end the therapy during her time in DC, never returning to my consulting room in London. This troubling and unsuccessful experience of giving therapy remotely made me feel particularly apprehensive about moving my patients from in-person to online sessions when the COVID pandemic struck. I'm relieved to say that, despite some hiccups, none of my current patients have ended their treatment as Scarlett did.

I poured another whiskey and observed that after the opened messages from Scarlett were pages of unopened spam, a record of bold nonsense from the 1990s which, as the multiple adverts for erectile dysfunction cures suggested, were not yet targeted through algorithms. I scrolled down, inanely, allowing the odd archaic spam heading to hold my fuzzy gaze. I was about to stop and return to the top of the list to re-read our correspondence, when Scarlett Durand's name appeared in bold with the other unread items. I quickly entered her name into the search box and a list of further unread emails appeared; the first in 1998, the last in 2010. Two had Word documents attached to them, the first titled *Umbilical Cord* and the second *Handmaids*, words that for me were pregnant with anxiety about the possibility of forgetting a patient, despite my usual thoroughness.

That sinking feeling brewed in my stomach, the foreboding sense that arises in a recurring dream I often have where I'm looking after someone else's baby while driving down a motorway and notice that the infant is unusually quiet. I glance in the rear-view mirror to check that the baby is alright and find the back seat empty, the baby and its carrier gone. In that moment, I remember that I set the baby carrier down on the floor of a petrol station when I refuelled the car, miles back. I know I have already left the baby for far too long in a dangerous place and frantically look for somewhere I can exit the motorway, turn around and go back to save it. But the road stretches on endlessly and I cannot stop or turn off, all I can do is continue to speed away from the baby I should be looking after. If only I had checked the inbox occasionally to see if Scarlett had tried to make contact. I should have anticipated that she would use the email address to try to repair the damage she did in DC. But Scarlett's calling out to me for thirteen years after, in my mind at least, the therapy had ended, had gone unanswered and unheard. She had been forgotten until an automated message prompted me to remember her.

What follows is the emails between myself and Scarlett while she was in Washington DC, her subsequent messages to me and their attachments, my long-awaited reply to her, and the unexpected correspondence that resulted from it.

Hannah Kublitz
5th January 2021

Part I: Washington DC Emails
June 1997 – August 1997

. . . [P]sychoanalysis would not have been what it was (any more than so many other things) if E-mail, for example, had existed. And in the future, it will no longer be what Freud and so many psychoanalysts have anticipated, from the moment E-mail . . . became possible.

Jacques Derrida, *Archive Fever* (1995)

03/06/1997

Hi Hannah,

It feels strange to be writing to you, almost illicit.

    I dreamt about the mystery woman again last night. We're in a room, my room, I think, in this dream. The woman looks different today. Today she's in a different body. She's a circus performer swathed in a skin of shiny leopard-print lycra. Her hair is cropped, spiked, bleached blond. She moves deftly around this room which, although she is off-duty, is her ring and I am her audience. There's little in the room, which is located in the basement of an institutional building. I'm pleased, excited even, to have the woman in my room. I know that she is there only for me. Time collapses and the woman is on the other side of the room. I think she might have back-flipped there. This makes me laugh, but only inside. I don't want to embarrass the woman who seems not to have realised that she is in this other, inappropriate, body. I want to hold the moment. The woman lies back against the wall. I notice the roundness of her breasts, the artificial toning of her body. I then realise that the woman is an artifice, that she is slipping away. I look at the woman and think that I want to touch her before the illusion dissolves completely. The woman looks back at me from the floor, as though she might want the same. As if to justify my actions, I say 'this is a dream'. With a look, I tell the woman that I'm going to kiss her. The woman closes her eyes and I lean down towards her, but as I do I go blind. It is as though the woman has shut my eyes too. My lips move through the darkness expectantly. I imagine how the woman might feel, what the sensation of reaching into her mouth might be like. I'm at the woman's lips now but I can't feel them. I reach forwards, inwards, but there is only darkness. The woman's mouth is an abyss in which I find myself lost.

My waking life is far more banal, I'm afraid. I arrived in DC on Friday and my first day of research in the Margaret Mead Papers and South Pacific Ethnographic Archives was yesterday. The archive is not what I expected: No cobwebs, no darkness, no getting dusty while rummaging through piles of boxes, as I had fantasised. There are very strict rules. After you've passed through security checks at the grand main entrance to the Library of Congress's Madison Building which include bag scans, passing through metal detectors and sometimes being frisked by uniformed men with guns, you make your way through the nineteenth century statues to the locker room at the entrance to the Manuscript Reading Room. Here you must leave all pens, papers, books, notepads or anything that might allow you to mark or to conceal an archival document. Once you've done this, yet another security guard checks you are free of any offending items before you can enter the Manuscript Reading Room (MRR) itself. You then make your way to the front desk to have your ID badge checked and are allocated a desk; the desks are arranged a good distance apart from each other as if to prevent cheating in an exam. Of course this immediately makes me feel inclined to cheat, but at what I'm not sure.

Despite all the high-security, it is a shiny, red star-sticker that a librarian placed on my ID badge, like the kind you would give a school child for good behaviour, that proves I have 'Kluge Scholar' status and can therefore look at any items I choose from the archive. You request the boxes of items from an alphanumerical catalogue and an archivist brings them to you on a trolley.

It's cold and window-less in the MRR, like a morgue. I long to sit outside the front of the building, smoking in the early-summer sun, but of course I'm not allowed to take any documents out there, and I can't easily pop out for a break as I'd have to pass through all the security checks to get back in again. It seems that for the next nine months I will spend most of my days confined to cold storage.

I'd better get on with my work. I'll write again next week.

Scarlett

04/06/1997

Good Morning Scarlett,

Thank you for your E-mail. I wonder what the connection might be between your dream about this 'different' version of mystery woman and your arrival in the archive that is unlike you expected, and produces this different, 'almost illicit', experience of therapy.

You are perhaps anxious that being in 'a morgue' could be, like the woman's mouth, an abyss in which you will become lost. But I notice you write you will 'find' yourself lost and perhaps through this solitary journey into the archive, you also hope to find out something new about yourself. Are you, like the mystery woman, 'different' in this new place, and if so, will this new version of yourself be impressive and capable or (I'm thinking of the back-flip) inappropriate, laughable and embarrassing, provoking uncomfortable feelings?

You are afraid that your waking life is 'far more banal' than your dream life, and this comment perhaps speaks to your need to reflect your parents' 'specialness'; to perform, entertain, thrill, seduce, provoke, but never to bore, or disappoint, or else (what?).

I attach my invoice for May.

With best wishes,
Hannah

10/06/1997

Hi again,

You assume the mystery woman in a dream-version of myself, but I don't know if that's right. Perhaps there's something here about identification and desire and an assumption on your part that one's feeling towards someone of the same gender must 'naturally' be to identify with them rather than to desire them. Couldn't it be that I desire her rather than identify with her? Or could it be both? Would it be narcissistic if it were both?

So this morning I had a coffee, two cigarettes and I opened a lovely E-mail from my mum which, after detailing her latest DIY project and social escapades, asked how 'Margaret' (Mead) and I are doing, followed by several rows of kisses. I had to confess that archive fever seems to be contagious and that I have been obsessively recording how Mead obsessively recorded everything, and that I suspect I may soon get neuritis, as she did. There I go identifying with Margaret...

I have my routine sorted now: Up at 6.15, shower first (I have to wait for my hair to dry before leaving as there's no hairdryer), breakfast, tea, fag, get my stuff together. I leave my cute little 'artist's apartment' in Kenwood at 7.30am and walk five minutes to the bus stop on Wisconsin Avenue. There I get the 31, 32 or 36 bus to Foggy Bottom metro which passes through Georgetown and takes about twenty minutes. At Georgetown I get on the Blue or Orange line to

Capitol South (eight stops I think), which takes about fifteen mins. I almost feel like a local.

I keep coming across these intriguing notes in little chequebook-esque pads. They are so seductive, little slips of tracing paper like little slips of thought, slippages. This one reads:

```
Social comment | March 20
Ngidep, taking through a yard and stopping
to chatter a minute in the doorway of a house
where I Janti and Men Djadeng were making
offerings. Ngidep said: "This is a borrowed
house, these are latjoer people"
```

These slips of paper are like playing cards or fragments of film, all disjointed and unnumbered yet each bound in its own perfect internal logic. Here's another:

```
I Doeras | March 21
Wandered in all alone with a long folded piece
of paper in his mouth, thrust half down his
throat, asking me for medicine for a sore.
Given some marbles he carried them away,
opened the paper and put them inside, and de-
parted, as disconnectedly as he had come.
```

I like that each slip has been removed entirely from its original context; as 'disconnected' as the Balinese people they describe.

This morning I am in good spirits, despite being worse

for wear after last night's bottle of wine while on the phone to Fran, which was a lighter, easier conversation than I had expected. It was as though time rewound and we'd never got together, we'd just stayed good friends. But Fran is a scientist in the conventional sense, she doesn't get my work. We bond over our shared love of dogs, wine, scrabble and vintage clothing but I need to avoid those sorts of distractions to keep focussed on my project to understand what Mead and Bateson's Balinese research really demonstrates about the relationship between mothering and the development of schizophrenia (if anything).

I've asked my mum to put a cheque in the post to you to cover your invoice.

Until next week.
Scarlett

11/06/1997

Good morning Scarlett,

It is an interesting question you ask about identification and desire. I wonder if, when you imagine I would see your desire for a same-sex object as narcissistic or 'unnatural', this is an anxiety you have about yourself?

These slips or fragments are removed from their original context, as are you. You say there is something 'seductive' about them and perhaps that links to your feeling that writing to me rather than seeing me in the consulting room is an 'almost illicit' experience. Can the boundaries be maintained here, outside the walls of the consulting room?

I also notice that the first slip mentions a 'borrowed house' and I wonder if your recounting of your morning routine and journey from your apartment to the Library of Congress is an attempt to make your new life in DC feel less borrowed and more 'yours', to anchor yourself in this new context.

Best wishes,
Hannah

17/06/1997

Hi Hannah,

Well, you do feel more seductive over E-mail than in person. Maybe that's because over E-mail you are less defined so I can read more of my own 'thrilling', 'seductive' self into your words. I agree with you about wanting to anchor myself in this context, I want to feel 'at home' here, that I belong rather than am living a borrowed life. Nine months, well, eight and a half now, is a long time to feel like a visitor. I notice that there is an area of DC near my apartment called 'Friendship Heights'. Maybe I should go there and stick my thumb out, see if I can 'hitch' myself a friend.

It is strange that all my friendships, all my relationships, are now conducted through electronic means – phone or E-mail. I suppose I should be grateful that I'm not reliant on letters; in Mead's correspondence there are many misunderstandings and heart aches because of letters not being delivered on time, or at all, particularly between her and her long-term lover, Ruth Benedict, by whom she often worries she has been rejected.

When Mead went to Bali, she had recently married Gregory Bateson, having been married twice before, but her relationship with Benedict was constant throughout her marriages. Benedict was Mead's mentor, almost fifteen year her senior, also an anthropologist and, from the impression the letters between them give, she was softer, kinder and less neurotic than Mead. They write to each other so lovingly, tenderly, with letters beginning 'my darling' and going on to reference their shared love of particular poems, psychoanalysis, and of course anthropology. Mead becomes terribly anxious when she thinks Benedict has not replied to one of her letters. As Mead kept a carbon copy of everything she ever wrote, it seems, the full correspondence between them (and everyone else with whom Mead corresponded by letter) is present in the archive. It's an odd mix of the trials of her personal life and her research, and I can't help reading one into the other.

Anyway, I'm in the MRR as usual, looking at box N11, folder 1, today, in which there is more notes, some in Balinese. Folder 2 yields much of the same. Later, there are pages with their corners turned upwards. I wonder why a researcher has done this. The pages with the corners turned up for photocopying bear little difference to the rest as far as I can tell. Perhaps the researcher who did this was a specialist in the region so could make meaning of all this ethnographic detail. It seems beautiful in form but devoid of any significant content to me. I like some of the phrases, a lot of them in fact but, again, taken out of context. Here it is only possible to read them out of context.

Further on the notes become much more descriptive and eloquently written, in paragraphs, not numerical note form. However, I'm much more interested in the 'slips' and my mind keeps coming back to these. There is some connection between these fragments of writing and film clips, something more than them just being 'clips', but I can't work out what it is. Last night I tried reading them aloud, listening to how the numbers interrupt the words arbitrarily. It felt like there was some value to this, reading these 'dead' pages aloud, resurrecting them in a way. Perhaps it could lead to a sound piece about the surreal qualities of fieldwork and my over-production of records in this archive-field which seems to mirror Mead's.

Here's another appealing slip:

```
                    ? MK
Can a girl who is not a daa dance the redjang?
As a substitute?
If all the daas are dancing?
Does a daa who is a redjang have ti send a
substitute if she can't dance?
If a daa who is sebel, fined for not tedoen ing?
Must she send a substitute or be fined?
```

In box N7, folder 6 there is a page headed 'Diary April 1936' in which there are reams of notes with each line numbered in the margin, arbitrarily it appears. This format is repeated on almost every page until I get to one on which the numbers are scribbled over and partially re-ordered, with a note saying 'Each date starts with No.1'. What does this mean? In the next folder there are endless pages with indecipherable markings. Many of the notes are handwritten. No wonder Mead developed neuritis.

The man at the desk in front of me is being reprimanded for having more than one folder on his desk at a time. The librarian comes to my desk next. I blush. What have I done now? She asks me if I'm still using the guide, a large lever-arch file detailing the entire Margaret Mead Papers.

Have I kept it too long? I reply to her 'Well yes, but not right at this minute so if someone else wants to use it that's fine'. The librarian says no, it is just because I can't order any more boxes now as it's too close to closing, so why do I need it? I tell her I have it here just to help reference what I'm looking at. She seems satisfied with that. I keep the guide and hope she isn't looking over my shoulder as I write this.

Scarlett

18/06/1997

Good morning Scarlett,

You say that you find yourself reading the personal life of the researcher into her research, and perhaps you are inviting me to do the same with you. These E-mails seem to be becoming a repository for your research findings as much as a space for you to work through the 'trials and tribulations' of your own personal life.

Before you left for DC, you were preoccupied with your thoughts and feelings about whether your relationship with Fran would end permanently, or would be on pause while you were away and could be resumed when you return to London, but there is little mention of that relationship here. Similarly, your intense and at times almost unbearable feelings about your mother's illness are absent in your recent correspondence, as is your working through of traumatic experiences in your early life, which were a large part of the therapy before you left for DC. It seems that the 'content' of your personal life is left out of this E-mail therapy, but maybe played out through your reading of the archive. I wonder what you make of that and whether you feel it would be possible to share your thoughts and feelings about your personal life more explicitly with me in this correspondence?

Best wishes,
Hannah

24/06/1997

Hi Hannah,

I feel like you're telling me off for not sharing my private life as freely here as I would in the room. But I think that is a tall order when I'm using the same laptop for these E-mails that I do to write up my research, and there's no shared experience of being in the same place together. Here I'm at a remove from everything that was familiar to me, from my old life (yes, I already think of it as my 'old' life), and from myself. I need you to follow me into this new, solitary life in the archive, or I think I may become lost altogether and never find my way back. I'll try to put myself into these E-mails more explicitly, but please don't stop looking for me in the research material.

As I write these words, I see Mead's in front of me. `'DON'T DESTROY ANYTHING ANYTHING ANYTHING'` is the last line of folder R15, which contains Mead's instructions for what should be done with her works and personal effects after her death. In the four pages of instructions, written to a presumably unknown reader, Mead refers to herself in the third person `'After her death, Margaret's papers and films are to be moved from the Institute for Intercultural Studies and held at the Library of Congress'`, for example. She clearly views herself as a far superior archivist to her husband, of whom she writes, in the same file, `'Never give him the last copy of anything'`.

Mead's writing about herself in the third person reminds me of a game I used to play as a child; an only child, as you know. I would sit on my bed and say my name over and over again until the syllables became disorientated, consonants distorted, and the vowels began to run in unfamiliar directions. I'd move from being a first to a third person. Playing the game used to frighten me but I felt compelled to repeat it. It was similar to the experience of watching back the home movies my father made of me. I would often watch the precariously flickering VHS tapes of myself and was always keen for more to be made. Though I haven't seen the films since my teens, I have a clear memory of the events that take place in many of them. However, I often find that I can't distinguish between my genuine memories of taking part in the events depicted on screen, and my memories of watching myself as an actor in them at a later date. My first-person experiences of birthdays, picnics, seaside trips and other filmable occasions has been overwritten by their on-screen version. Rather than remembering my first-person experiences in those scenarios, I am rotated to the position of third person, as a witness to my screen-self. Perhaps this sort of 'making strange' is what later drew me to the surrealists, and to ethnography's inverse project of making the strange familiar. Scrutinizing one's own name, screen image, or reflection, as if it belonged to another, has an uncanny effect. Maybe therapy is a little like that too, but you will think I'm 'intellectualising' again.

There are literally thousands of boxes that I couldn't possibly go through in the time I'm here. Despite all this formal alphanumerical ordering, when you actually come to take the thin, typewritten pages out of the storage boxes, many of them read like surrealist poetry. Here are some from the box of notes headed 'March 1936' which I'm looking at now. The first one references Walter Spies who was a gay artist living in Bali when Mead and Bateson were there, as many artists and writers did at the time. He was arrested for 'homosexuality' at the start of the war and deported on a ship which sank with all the 'criminals' still locked in their cells on the lower deck. It makes section 28 look like a picnic! Anyway, I digress:

```
Girls dancing at Walter's village a failure
because it was real honest behavior
No Double twist

Casual Impersonal suckling develops into
Esophagal type or orality
Highly developed

Great.
Possibility that people assimilate zones.
Limbs
```

```
Evening wrote letter to Ruth
Sent off mail to Ruth, Steve, Eliz, Monte,
Helt, Max, Fluffy
Restless night expecting birth.
```

```
Morning paper from village on Djassar
When Sebatoe road branches
Series of
            Movements along in pairs
                    frogs
                    dogs
        one black one,
one (old) woman with pronounced clitoris
        a pregnant woman
        a large old child suckling
Refused our prices
Watched cock fight,
Bet Bonjo woman,
Did cremation,
Visited little Karbo and all.
Said Neloeboelanin for his child in 12 days
```

```
Infants have a limp waxy character,
Children respond to flirting – not to warmth.
People do not smile
Continual play on in theatre.
The buttocks is regarded as a limb.
Extraordinary amount of farting.
```

```
Entering between the two umbrellas.
Witchy step, lowering the body and lowering
```

```
the arms at the same time.
Genital emphasis produced by the springiness
in the knee.
Enter the ugly daughter,
Made up face, and long anteng, hand in hooked
position.
Outstretched arms and bent knee repeats.
```

What does 'Neloeboelanin' mean? What is an 'anteng'? Who is the ugly daughter? How do I analyse these notes to make any sort of critique of Mead and Bateson's study of the 'schizophrenic' Balinese character?

Sorry, I'm feeling overwhelmed today.

Scarlett

25/06/1997

Good morning Scarlett,

I notice you imagine that through playing your name repeating game, like watching back your home movies, you will move from the first to the third person which, in the latter case, is actually your father's position and not an objective one. What about the second person? Another mind who might see you, and with whom you might relate and interact? I think you are saying that the second person, that I, seem very remote to you at the moment, part of your 'old' life, but that you feel you need me to hold onto you in order for you to maintain yourself and not become lost in this new place you find yourself in.

It's interesting that after seeming to step back into a third position you quote Mead's 'surrealist poems' which are very visceral and bodily. The images that stand out to me from the excerpts you have chosen to send are the large old child suckling, pronounced clitoris, extraordinary amount of farting, and outstretched arms. Are you locating your more infantile needs and impulses in the archive's ethnographic subjects while you struggle to remain a shiny, independent, screen-worthy version of yourself, as you felt you had to appear to your parents as a child?

Best wishes,
Hannah

01/07/1997

Hi Hannah,

I think it's a bit much to claim that I'm projecting my unwanted needs into the Balinese, though I think that's what Mead and Bateson, and other anthropologists at the time, might have been doing. But I think you are right that I find it hard to imagine that there is a 'second person', a 'you', there to receive my communications, by E-mail at least. Easier to imagine it's just my reflection in the mirror, or else I'm a third person looking in from the outside, as I am in this archive, I suppose - an Oedipal interloper getting between Mead and Bateson maybe? I have to confess that I do find myself looking for cracks in their relationship and wishing Mead would run off with Ruth Benedict, with whom I do identify.

Related to this, I found a note about Maya Deren (a very sexy avant-garde filmmaker active in the 1940s & 50s) in Mead's archive today which says that some of the Balinese films were made by her... This seems very unlikely as she would only have been just nineteen when they set off for Bali in 1936. Anyway, my interest was piqued as an avant-garde filmmaker seems an unlikely candidate to be connected with Mead and Bateson 'scientific' study for purely professional purposes. Was she sleeping with Margaret, or Gregory, or both of them? The cataloguing card for these films in the Motion Picture Division says (with typos uncorrected):

```
JH telephoned JVV 9/16/71

Re: Maya Deren Film JVV

MM said that this film is made of
bits of cuts from Balinese films that
were filmed by MD & lent to her by
Gregory Bateson. She used them to
make up new cuts & was to return
them to their original place which
she never did.
They are to be treated like all other
Balinese films in storage, payment,
etc. JVV knows the procedure. There
should be numbers referring to the
Bali films. MM said that if it was
not obviously Balinese film that it
would be her Haiti films, in which
case it should be returned and nothing
done.
JVV said it seemed to be Balinese
filme & he would procede. He will
return the original here, which should
be stored with original Bali films.
He'll make a dupe neg. with frames
numbered & 2 pos. - 1 for EPPI and
one to be stored here.
```

'MM' is Margaret Mead and MD Maya Deren but I'm going to have to work out who 'JH' and 'JVV' are and follow this up…

 I had another dream about the mystery woman this week who, come to think of it, often looks quite like Maya Deren. The woman appears, this time in a body that is closer to her own. We are in an institutional building again, now in the corridors. I hope that this time the woman might kiss me. We keep walking. The carpets get deeper and the ceilings higher. We reach a ballroom filled with young revellers. I think they might be students at this institution. I can't remember what my place is here. Some kind of event is taking place, a performance of some sort, which I think the woman and I might be involved in, but I can't remember how. The people have theatrical costumes and props; branches, masks, donkeys' ears. Perhaps we are backstage.

The woman has a small digital camera that seems out of step with this place of another time. She gives me the camera and asks me to take pictures so that we can remember the event. The woman poses with a few of the raucous thespians. I hope that someone else will offer to take the camera so that I can be in the photographs with the woman. Again, I want to capture the moment. Nobody offers. I only want to photograph the woman but I know I must take photographs of the whole group if I am to please her. As I aim the camera at the group, more young women arrive into the frame, all in costumes from this other time. They start to dance in front of me, obscuring the woman and the group I was asked to photograph. The floor seems to extend itself, moving me away from my original position, away from the woman. Every now and then I catch a glimpse of her between the theatrical crowds. Now she is dancing. I'm surprised, I've never seen the woman dance like this, I've never seen her move so freely. I want to join in but I remember the camera. This shiny little out-of-step object prevents me from participating.

I think this will be the end of the dream, that the woman

will disappear into the crowds which will act as another abyss into which the moment dissolves. But the thespian crowds start to part and the woman walks directly towards me. She seems more present than ever. I can feel myself as if I am awake. I notice that there is a red bandana scarf open around my neck. The texture is unfamiliar; a chalky, starched cotton. It is not mine and I don't remember where it came from. 'Did you put this on me?' I ask the woman. As I speak this line, I remember that the woman lives with me now. In the same moment, I remember that earlier that day I had left our home wearing a more attractive, familiar, silk scarf. I think that perhaps the woman took the silk scarf from around my neck while I was napping and replaced it with the bandana scarf. I want to ask the woman about this but I forget my question in her smile and remember my desire to please her. The woman says that I had always been wearing that scarf and I believe her, although it contradicts my memory. I try to work out what I might be remembering wrongly but I'm distracted by the woman beginning to lead me away from the crowds as I awake.

Scarlett

02/07/1997

Good Morning Scarlett,

It is an interesting fantasy that you are an 'Oedipal interloper' in the archive, (perhaps like Maya Deren who resembles the mystery woman in your dreams?) and you might think more about how this connects with your earlier question about identifying with and desiring the same object.

The digital camera seems symbolic of your work in the archive, your tool in this 'new life' that stops you from participating in relationships at home, as the home movie camera in your childhood perhaps prevented a more genuine interaction between you and your parents. It feels like there is something performative in the E-mails you write to me, a performance of your academic prowess that gets in the way of a real, direct, connection with me and the other relationships you have left on the other side of the Atlantic. Something familiar (like the silk scarf), that has been replaced with something unfamiliar and you can't quite remember or make sense of how you/it got there.

I attach my invoice for June.

Best wishes,
Hannah

08/07/1997

Hi Hannah,

I think what you say is a bit harsh. Again, this idea that I'm 'performing', that I'm somehow fake, not genuine. It takes a lot to lay myself out in writing like this, but you don't seem to get that... When you write that sort of thing it makes me want to retreat into my research and talk even less explicitly about myself.

Anyway, my interest in the tactile qualities of the scarf might also be connected with my increasing interest in the visceral qualities of the archive. I find I'm excited not only by the crude descriptions of the bodies of the ethnographic subjects but also the 'bodily' qualities of the archive itself. In particular, I like the rust marks that old paperclips leave on the thin papers. In a notebook in folder 5 paper box N11 (sorry I can't stop with the archival precision!), clipped to the first page is what appears to be an order form for film/photographic materials titled 'N.V.FOTOTECHNISCH BUREAU EN HANDEL MIJ' - a Dutch company I imagine. Where it had been paper-clipped there is a single rust mark. Presumably it had been there since July 11th 1936, the date on the notebook. Now I've moved it, will a new rust mark be made over the next six decades it sits in the archive? The last notebook from this folder reveals another rusty paper clip on one of the middle pages, apparently superfluous. I photograph it and the mark it has made on the following page, then move it slightly for posterity and photograph my intervention. Am I messing with the archive? This is a deliberate transgression. The page tears slightly. Pleasure.

I'm going to move through yesterday's notes meticulously, photographing everything I made a note to photocopy. I've come to realise that, as one can bring a digital camera into the MRR and little else, the best way to make a record of what I am viewing in the archive is to photograph it. I photograph the box's and folder's alphanumerical references before their contents so that when I get back to my apartment in the evening I can download the photos and order them under the correct reference. I'm making a digital archive of the physical archive, but I'm still not sure what for... I feel like I'm losing sight of what I originally came here to research and getting lost in the archive. Maybe I've got 'archive fever' – ha! I'm going to re-read Derrida's book *Archive Fever: A Freudian Impression* which came out two years ago and has been getting a lot of attention in my field. It's about the relationship between the archive, psychoanalysis and what Derrida calls 'technologies of inscription' (E-mail, for example). You might find it interesting.

The folder in front of me now contains slips of annotated paper, bound with string that slides off as I pull the books out of the folder. This is not a secure way to hold papers together. Some pages are typed, some handwritten. I dare to take off the string so I can read them. Am I allowed to do this? I don't think I'll be able to put it back on properly.

I was thinking about still life and how it seems natural to record these 'papers' as a series of still photographs, as if they were 'still life' left for me to paint by an art teacher, like a bowl of fruit. The archive is a still life, a corpse. Of course, it is also a still life in the sense of it being the static remains of Margaret's life. Or not so static – I am reminded of the paperclips.

In the next box, N15, are more of Bateson's notebooks. The first book is entitled `Running field notes…(includes pictures taken in Java, in September)` but there are no pictures. I flick through the notebooks in folders 1 and 2 to get a sense of what is there and find more of Bateson's indecipherable handwriting. In folder 3 there is a 'Medicine Book'. The book begins in a reasonably organized, coherent fashion, then descends into chaos, as most of Bateson's notebooks seem to.

Until next week.
Scarlett

09/07/1997

Good morning Scarlett,

Perhaps the destructive quality of your desires is coming to the fore – I am thinking of the paperclips and your feeling that you are 'messing with' (by which I think you also mean 'messing up', or destroying) the archive. Also present in your musings on the paperclips is a question about whether you will make a lasting mark on the archive, which may partly be to do with your anxiety about whether your research project will 'make a mark' in academia, but I'm also wondering if it is about whether this remote form of therapy can make a mark on your psyche. Can you 'lay yourself out' in writing, as you put it, or will you hide within your archival research?

You say you are becoming lost in the archive, and I wonder if you also mean that you are becoming lost in your own unconscious processes, less able to repress and rationalize feelings as you used to. This, I think, connects to what we communicated about in the session two weeks ago, which is how you are using your work in the archive to play out aspects of your internal world. It sounds like the line between what is yours, by which I mean a projection of your internal world, and what is there in the archive that might inform your research, is quite muddled for you at the moment.

On a more practical note, I'd like to let you know that the summer break will be during the last two weeks of

August so our last session before the break will be 12th August and we will resume on 2nd September.

Best wishes,
Hannah

15/07/1997

Hi again,

I can't really take in what you said in your last E-mail. I spoke to my mother last night and she has had more bad news; it looks like the cancer might have spread to her lymph nodes so she is going to have more tests. She says she has lost quite a bit of weight which isn't a good sign. She still sounds well in herself though, moaning about her 'dreadful' Tory neighbour, between sips of wine and drags on her cigarette. Then the sipping and inhaling goes quiet for a bit while she reconnects her nose to her oxygen tubes. And yes, I have warned her, more than once, not to smoke next to the oxygen tank but her usual response, since the cancer spread to her brain, is 'don't be mean to poor old cancer-head'. I've stopped mentioning it now.

After I spoke to my mum on the phone I had this horrible creeping, guilty, feeling about being in DC when she is home in London, sick, and having to go to tests with friends rather than with me. Then I had this strange and intense dream about the woman which I woke up almost high on. I wonder what you will think of it. The mystery woman and I are walking down the institutional corridor again, heading back to my room. The woman has become more tender and her hair has grown. She puts her hand on the small of my back and I am excited and relieved. I know that the woman now loves me. An upwards escalator brings my mother into the corridor and the woman and I stop to greet her.

My mother is younger, her hair long and crimped like she used to wear it when I was a child. She knows that the woman and I are going home to bed. The woman leans forward to kiss my mother goodnight. I watch intently as the woman puts her left hand around my mother's neck and kisses her on the mouth. As she does so the woman moves her right hand along my back, and I almost know that it is not my mother, but me, whom the woman means to kiss. I kiss my mother's cheeks goodnight and as we begin to move away the woman cups her hand around my wrist, as though this form of embrace were absolute. I respond by moving my fingers upwards to feel the woman's knuckles and am comforted. In the same moment I move out of my body and watch myself and the woman disappear down the corridor.

I'm finding it increasingly difficult to make a path through this archive. I try to choose, from their somewhat cryptic titles, which of the thousands of boxes here might contain documents that are relevant to my project, which might reveal Mead and Bateson's underlying assumptions about the effects of child-rearing in Bali on the development of the so-called 'schizophrenic' Balinese character. However, as Mead and Bateson's whole project was to examine how 'pathogenic' mothering in Bali led to the development of a 'schizophrenic' character, which they thought they could be directly translated to understand the development of the then growing number of schizophrenics in institutions in the US, it is difficult to narrow it down.

A colleague once said to me 'never choose a bad object of study', and I think I have done just that. I'm here, really, hoping to debunk Mead and Bateson's work; to show how their project pathologized mothers and others and was far from the 'objective' study it purported to be. I've set myself in opposition to the archive in which I must be immersed for nine months.

By the way, you didn't mention Derrida's *Archive Fever*. Are you going to read it? I really hope you will.

Scarlett

16/07/1997

Good morning Scarlett,

I am sorry to hear that you mother's condition may be worsening.

Vis-à-vis the dream about the mystery woman in which your mother appears; I think it needs to be understood in the light of what came before it, namely the possibility that your mother's cancer may have spread again and your guilt about being away during this time. Are you perhaps hoping to share some of your youth and vitality with your mother? In the dream you transform her into her younger, healthier self and, in a sense, you share some of your excitement and zest for life (manifest in the figure of the mystery woman in this particular dream, I think) with her. This gift of youth and health is perhaps a way of reducing your guilt at not being there in-person to support her. I notice that at the end of the dream you move out of your body and watch yourself and the woman disappear, so you are rotated to the position of a third person again. It is noticeable that this disembodiment (or dissociation, perhaps?) happens after an embrace that feels 'absolute' and after you say you are 'comforted'. Are you perhaps attempting to escape the intimacy of an 'absolute' embrace and the feeling of comfort (or dependency?) that comes with it?

It is an interesting observation you make that you have chosen a 'bad object of study' and I wonder what it means for you to be 'in opposition' to it. I also notice you will be 'immersed in' (and in opposition to) this archive about 'pathogenic' mothering for a pregnant term of nine months...

Best wishes,
Hannah

22/07/1997

Hi again Hannah,

I'm not sure about your interpretation of my dream. I think it's more about whether I will get my mother's approval to move on and be with a partner after her death, especially with a woman rather than a man. Although she won't admit it because she thinks of herself as a progressive (which she is in many ways) and believes that 'everyone is bisexual', I know my mother would prefer that I ended up with a male partner. 'Being with a woman is fine when you're in your twenties darling, but what about when you want to have your babies?' She always says *your* babies, as though they already exist in a parallel universe and are just waiting to enter my womb and pass through my vaginal canal. Maybe I want my mother's blessing to be with someone like the mystery woman, and have babies (or not), with her. Maybe I wonder whether my mother thinks I will be a 'pathogenic' mother, and I wonder that about myself too.

I'm in the manuscript reading room, as usual at 10am on Tuesdays, or 3pm UK time, as I try to follow your rule of writing to you at our usual session time. I'm looking at box N14 which yields more of Bateson's notebooks, very similar to those that came before... I have just been reprimanded by a librarian for having moved the box from the trolley to the table. I did so to prop open one of the pages of the notebooks. Oops. It actually wasn't an intentional transgression this time, I just forgot. The reprimanding librarian offered to supply me with an alternative prop.

Now I've gone back to looking at box N10. The first three folders are the small chequebook-esque notebooks. They look beautiful from above, like the crumpled leaves of a tiny, ancient book. I want to photograph them but I remember I'm not supposed to take the boxes off the trolley (which sits by my desk), only the individual files. I can't reach to take a photo from above without moving the box. I transgress and move the box quickly onto my desk, snap, snap, nobody notices, box back on trolley. Safe.

In box N10, folder 4, there are more notes on thin paper. I photographed 'preliminary social organization survey' mainly because I like the layout. This stuff is not interesting. On to N11. All the notes in this box are so dense and each folder is bursting with them. Oh, I just missed a book under 'unclassified morphemes' titled 'Human slips' - how great! That reminds me that yesterday I saw the same cheque-book-esque pads with other titles such as 'slippages', or 'corpses': Are corpses a kind of human slip? I'm also thinking of them as Freudian slips of course, which they are in several senses.

Here are some of my favourite type-written entries from inside the notepad entitled 'human slips':

```
Ngenges = nasal secretions
Not a polite word but there is no other

Pedjoeh = semen
Same word used for female secretions
```

One wonders how Gregory Bateson explained to the (presumably non-English-speaking) Balinese which parts of the body he wanted to know the words for...

I'll leave you with that thought.

Scarlett

23/07/1997

Good morning Scarlett,

On some level you might feel your sexuality, your attraction towards women, is a kind of 'slip'? You quote the slip that says 'same word for female secretions [as male]' and this perhaps connects to your mother's seemingly contradictory claim that we are all bisexual but that a male partner would have more value to you in reproductive terms. You would prefer she held the Balinese view of male and female secretions being the same, by which I mean, of equal value.

You've expressed an anxiety that your future mothering may be 'pathogenic' (and it is unclear whether this concern is linked to judgements you imagine your mother and other people might make about same-sex parenting), but I wonder whether there is also some concern in you that you have received 'pathogenic', or less than ideal, mothering, and an anxiety about the impact that may have had on you.

You seem very preoccupied with the rules of the archive and your transgression of them, intentional or otherwise. Perhaps you wonder whether you make 'Freudian slips' in your correspondence with me and what they might expose about you. Does your correspondence have to be kept neat and controlled as any 'slips' you make give me access to areas of your internal world that you want to keep restricted?

Best wishes,
Hannah

29/07/1997

Hi Hannah,

It sounds quite belittling to suggest that my sexuality is a kind of 'slip'. That's not how I feel about it, that's how I think my mother (and maybe you!) feel about it. I don't know what to think about the question of mothering - me as a mother, my mother's mothering (which I think on the whole was very good and *not* pathogenic). I am acutely aware that I have a womb and a vagina but I don't want to use them in the way most women seem to. I don't know if I really want to identify with the category 'woman' at all but I'm not 'man' either, and what else is there to be? If you are right about one thing it is my preoccupation with restrictions and possible transgressions of them. I see restrictions everywhere in the archive.

Right now I'm looking at boxes P26-8 which have 'restricted' written on them. I noticed that there is a whole section of the Mead Papers that is 'restricted' when I went through the guide for the first time. Of course I asked the librarian why this particular section is restricted and if the restriction could be lifted under any circumstances. He said it would demand contacting Mead's daughter, Mary Catherine Bateson, who placed these particular documents under restriction quite recently apparently, and that I should talk to the head archivist about it. It's hard to make a case for needing to look at them when I don't know what's in them of course. The real reason I want to look at them (purely because they have been restricted and I like secrets) will not get me access to them, I suspect.

I need to look at every box from N7-N39 which is the Balinese section of the South Pacific Ethnographic archives. That's 32 boxes, 4 boxes per order, that's 8 orders and I reckon 2 hours per order (30 minutes per box). So I get 8 hours access time per day which, minus an hour for lunch and an hour for faffing, is 6 hours per day. 16 (let's call it 18) divided by 6 is 3, so it should take me 3 days to get through, that's until the end of this week. Ok, so this week I go through the ethnographic work and get it all covered and next week start on the personal correspondences and 'miscellaneous' folders, as well as contacting the other divisions, especially the Motion Picture Division, that hold Mead's work. I'll do that on Saturday.

In box N7 are folders of loose notes, all on tracing paper, I guess carbon copies. Each file, of which there are about 4 per box, is full to the brim. As I begin turning through the thin pages all I see is numbered lists of people and precise maps of house. The names are in print, there are handwritten notes next to them like 'D2-29-31'. I wish I could remember the anthropology kinship-code I learnt as an undergraduate so I could decipher the kin diagrams. At the back of the next folder is an A3 page, folded into 4 on square-lined paper, discoloured like the 'ancient maps' I used to make out of paper stained with tea as a child.

In box N16 are the same notebooks as in other boxes but I notice that each of them has a small, brown envelope stuck to the back page. I find each one is empty until I get to this one in folder 3. At first, as I check it, I see nothing, but then, when I squeeze my fingers in, fearing I may rip the paper and everyone in the Manuscript Reading Room will hear, I feel something shiny. I pull out the shiny square and find it is a black and white photograph of a topless Balinese woman. I wonder how she managed to stay snug in her envelope while the other women were syphoned off and filed in the photographic section of the archive.

I had another dream about the woman a few nights ago which is also about restrictions and slips, in a way. I walk across the fields of my college past a group of archers and am jolted by the mystery woman appearing, unexpectedly, from the other side of a bush. Today the woman is very serious. She is young with dark red hair and her clothes are grey and formal. 'I need to talk to you about your project,' she tells me, without first greeting me. 'Meet me at 3 o'clock.' Before I have time to respond, the woman has disappeared. I keep walking. Time and space collapse and I'm no longer walking on soft grass but on the rugged gravel at the front of the college, which grinds into my soles. A different, more likeable, version of the woman appears. She is also young but her face is softer, kinder and charged with emotion. The woman's eyes smile as she sees me. We almost laugh with joy at the sight of each other. The woman has bobbed black hair with a fringe and large, round eyes. She wears a long black coat that tapers tightly at the waist then flares, sweeping a large circumference of the ground surrounding her. Stitched into the exterior of the coat are vertical lines of scrap metal, off-cut materials, broken clock mechanisms and other outmoded paraphernalia. She hugs me and says 'Do not listen to anything the other woman will tell you at 3 o'clock. You can meet me instead to talk about your project if you like. I will leave it up to you.' With that the woman turns and I notice that stitched onto the back of her coat is a huge old rag doll whose feet sweep the floor as the woman bounds away. I decide that I far prefer this incarnation of the woman to the previous stern one, and am immediately transported through time and space to the alternative 3 o'clock meeting she offered me.

There, I find myself standing on a precipice at the edge of the college's fields. A solid old stone wall shields me from the drop below as the second incarnation of the woman appears. She has unpicked some of the old silk material stitched to the back of her coat's collar and wears it across part of her face. The woman's features are distorted yet still recognisable; the black silk obscures her cheeks and forms a strange addition to her elegance by being tied in a precise knot between her nose and her lips. 'I'm not going to give you any orders,' she says. 'I just want to tell you that you are inside me.' I am dumbstruck and I begin to feel embarrassed. 'Do you know how much this means to me?' Asks the woman. My silence speaks that I do not. 'Maybe this will tell you how much.' The woman hands me a wrapped tampon which I unwrap, tentatively. On the over-sized white cotton bullet is my E-mail address detailed in blue ink in my own small handwriting. I want to be flattered but I don't understand what this gesture means. I don't remember writing on the tampon and understand that the woman does not mean to say I ever did. I fear that the woman may have taken things too far, made them too base, too bodily. At this first truly visceral moment, the woman begins to dissolve again and I think that I must take advantage of this moment of intimacy offered to me by her. I put out my hand attempting to cup the woman's neck but, as I do so, the woman turns away. I intend to kiss the woman but it is too late. I begin to wake, doubting that I will ever see this incarnation of the woman again. If you can decipher that you deserve a medal!

There's another box of Mead's field notes on my desk but I have absolutely no desire to look through this box or the next. Mead's dense and seemingly endless fieldnotes have become like a dull radio programme twittering on in the background (that reminds me of how my mum used to listen to radio 4 endlessly when I was a child). I feel much more drawn to Derrida's slim but exciting book on the form of the archive, on the archival drive which is connected to Freud's death drive, and now it is framing the way I view everything here. It's a world apart in style and content from Mead's work but one connection is that *Archive Fever: A Freudian Impression* is in conversation with the historian Yerushalmi's *Freud's Moses: Judaism Terminable and Interminable* which is in conversation with Freud's *Moses and Monotheism* which he was re-writing for publication in 1936-8, the same time that Mead and Bateson were in Bali making this archive. Another connection is that The Sigmund Freud Archives are also held here, at the Library of Congress, but they are restricted, or inaccessible to academics at least. I wonder what Derrida's take on that would be. I read *Archive Fever* aloud to myself in the evening sometimes, like a thrilling bedtime story.

I did ask you explicitly some time ago whether you're going to read *Archive Fever*, but you still haven't answered me. I think it would really help you to understand where I'm coming from and it asks (but doesn't answer) how psychoanalysis would have been different if Freud and his colleagues, rather than corresponding by letter, had corresponded by E-mail, which Derrida describes as a new 'technology of archivization'. He doesn't ask how psychoanalysis would have been different if analysts/therapists treated their patients via E-mail. Maybe that seemed a ridiculous or impossible idea to him, but here we are...

On to the drudgery of box N17 now.

Scarlett

30/07/1997

Good morning Scarlett,

My thoughts on your continuing preoccupation with restrictions and your attraction to secrets: Is it about wanting to intrude into 'restricted' areas of the other, as an oedipal interloper perhaps and/or is it about a desire to and a fear of accessing, 'restricted' areas of yourself in therapy?

The dream you share is, perhaps, a case in point. The line 'if you can decipher that you deserve a medal' feels like something of a test or challenge for me, which perhaps reflects the challenges you are experiencing in the seemingly 'indecipherable' archive. What stands out to me about the dream is the 3 o'clock meeting (the same time as our sessions) and the two versions of the woman; the first buttoned up and restrictive, leaving you longing for more, the second liberated and visceral as you had longed for, but leaving you feeling overwhelmed and 'dumbstruck'. But I wonder what you make of the dream?

I don't agree that it would be helpful to you for me to read *Archive Fever* but the reflections you have about yourself that might arise from, or be connected to, the book I am open to hearing. My thoughts on what you say in this most recent E-mail: You make a connection between Mead's 'dull' or 'twittering' archive and your mother when you were a child. I wonder if the more 'exciting' Derrida with his 'slim' book is symbolic of your father and his rather minimal yet somehow thrilling way of parenting when you were a child. You have said in earlier sessions that you feel guilty for, as a child, having openly preferred your 'exciting' father to your mother who was depressed at the time, and her comparatively 'dull', consistent, everyday parenting of you. This may also connect to how your parents seemed to you to be 'worlds apart' and you struggled to make sense of them together, as you do Mead and Derrida.

Just to confirm, the summer break will be during the last two weeks of August so our last session will be Tuesday 12th August and we will resume on 2nd September. I attach my invoice for July.

Best wishes,
Hannah

05/08/1997

Hannah,

It's very late in the day to tell me you are going on a break in two weeks, especially when you know the situation with my mother and with Fran - you know I'm going through a difficult time and that I have hardly anyone but you to rely on now. It feels callous, hurtful even, for you to suddenly leave me.

Your interpretation of the dream doesn't really ring true for me. So now the mystery woman is you? Two versions of my therapist? I think I said something important about gender, and feeling outside of what feels like its restrictive categories, but you don't say anything about that. Instead you go to male and female, mummy and daddy and I'm not sure I agree with your idea that Mead and Derrida are symbolic of my mum and dad, nor why you won't read *Archive Fever*. You are already conducting this therapy by reading my words, so why not Derrida's? His words feel more pertinent than anything I could write on this experience, or anything that you have so far. And now I wonder whether you will interpret that as an example of me being a simpering (or simmering) daddy's girl.

I don't feel inclined to share much today. Instead, I'm just going to copy and paste some of my field notes from this morning which paraphrase Mead's notes on a trance she and Bateson filmed that supposedly demonstrates the 'schizophrenic' nature of the Balinese.

The *Kris* dance is a ritual dance which the Balinese perform in a state of trance, or so they told anthropologists. A

Kris is a dagger with which the dancers stab themselves but without being cut because supposedly their state of trance protects them from injury. However, during this dance something goes wrong:

The group of *kris* dancers are dressed in white with red hibiscus in their hair. In unison they raise the *krisses* and look to the side, making a grunting noise, and then move into a patternized movement. At 11.34 Rawa comes out and immediately the line of men goes into trance. He's a curious, maladjusted, wetly eager person, fawning and hanging on Europeans as if culture-contact will provide the answer to his problems. Ordinarily his putty-like appearance makes him seem small, but in trance, with his hair down to his shoulder and bare to the waist, transfigured by the recent paroxism, he is a magnificent creature. He has been given two *krisses* with which he dances, piercing himself. There is blood showing on his chest, over the heart, and red smears on his white clothing. The men of the *kris* dance rush about Rawa and begin to suck the blood flowing from his wound. Rawa is picked up and taken into the temple seeming quite limp and unaware of what he is doing. They place him on a big stone in one of the shrines. He opens his eyes, gazes down at the wound from which the blood is spurting with each heartbeat. Other men with *krisses* who are also entranced run towards him and try to suck the blood away. One man has his mouth on the wound while a second licks around it wherever the blood trickles down. Those who are not entranced find red hibiscus leaves to stuff into the wound, pulling away the blood-sucking men in order to do this. Another man, Pemankoe, brings a handful of lime leaves which he crunches up in his mouth and stuffs in the wound. After he has given him aid in this way, Pemankoe yanks Rawa, literally trying to raise him up from his seat by the long hair on his head. He fails so takes the back of his hand and strikes him first on one cheek and then the other so that one could not see how Rawa could help but have two black eyes. Men begin to scream and cry while this is going on and the dancers standing nearest plead for Pemankoe to stop. But Pemankoe is either very much entranced himself, or else he has a private quarrel with Rawa, for he takes him by the nose and twists it into his face, then twists and pulls his ears, and punctuates all this with body and face blows while he keeps a steady string of incomprehensible language pouring forth.

On re-reading, I think I already know what you will make of that...

Scarlett

06/08/1997

Good morning Scarlett,

Perhaps you could think about why it is you want me to read words written by Derrida in order to understand you. What is it that you feel unable to say in your own words, and in your own name, about your experience in the archive?

Perhaps what you expect me to make of the event you paraphrase is that is that it symbolizes the aggression you feel towards me at the moment in what might be termed a 'private quarrel', or a 'ritualized dance' between us which you feel has 'gone wrong'. You maybe hoped that the therapy, (like the state of trance for the Balinese), would protect you from being wounded. At the moment I think you feel that you are bleeding out like Rawa, and I feel like Pemankoe who, first seems to be giving aid and then to be violently attacking.

It also puts me in mind of your comment early on in the therapy that my consulting room was like a vampire's lair; at the time you felt I was vulnerable and might be destroyed by the light outside but I think that has shifted in recent weeks and I perhaps feel like a more malign, attacking vampire who might hurt you and suck your blood, as in the tale you recount.

Apart from the connection with what is going on in the therapy, what also comes to mind for me when I read this very bloody story from the archive is your experience of haemorrhaging as a teenager which has had a significant, lasting impact on you. If I remember rightly, this traumatic event happened when you were abroad, a significant distance from your home (and your parents), as you are now. Given this, I wonder if, along with the aggression, you are communicating to me your ongoing need for containment during this time which you maybe feel you have lost with the cessation of in-person sessions, and will lose further with the up-coming break.

I hear that you are hurt, and that you feel I have been callous, but I did first give you the dates of the break four weeks ago, more than a month in advance of the break.

Best wishes,
Hannah

06/08/1997

Hannah,

I know I'm not meant to write to you outside our session time but I think this situation warrants it.

I looked back over our correspondence and I can see that, yes, you did send me your holiday dates four weeks ago. But I can also see that the first line I wrote in reply to your E-mail with the dates was 'I can't take in anything you said in your last E-mail' and that was because I'd just had bad news about my mother's health. One would hope that, as a therapist, you might be emotionally savvy enough to surmise that I therefore would not have absorbed the dates you sent me, and that you would therefore have sent them to me again soon after, not left it until the break is nearly upon us.

Maybe you are right about the connections with my teenage haemorrhaging incident but there doesn't seem to be time to go into that now. In effect you've opened a can of worms and I can't manage that on my own.

I've been thinking about it and, as our therapy is over E-mail anyway, do you really need to take a break? I mean even if you are going abroad you will surely have access to E-mail, so why the need to take time off? Can you please write back to me confirming that you will continue the E-therapy with me throughout August, and not take a break?

Scarlett

07/08/1997

Dear Scarlett,

I will keep this correspondence very brief as it outside of the bounds of our designated sessions.

I am sorry you feel that I neglected to make the dates of the break clear enough. However, they are fixed and, in order to maintain boundaries and containment for you, it will not be possible for us to have E-sessions during that time.

Kind regards,
Hannah

12/08/1997

Hannah,

I cried all day after reading your last E-mail refusing to see me during the holidays in such a cold, formal way: 'Dear Scarlett' and 'Kind regards', as if I'm an annoying business associate rather than someone who exposes their innermost thoughts and feelings to you.

It feels like we are out of synch, and these E-sessions are not only unhelpful to me, now they are actually becoming harmful.

I had another dream about the woman. I don't know whether to share it with you but maybe it says something important about the state of our relationship. It might be the last dream I share.

The woman pointed out a blackbird high up in the tree at the end of my garden. I had noticed it before but hadn't commented on it because I wasn't wearing contact lenses so could not be sure what it was. What we both noticed about the blackbird was its incongruous stillness. From its position, the blackbird appeared to be in mid-motion, wing bent, head turned down, but its position was fixed, its body devoid of all movement. It was as though the blackbird was frozen in a still blackbird-shaped frame at the centre of a moving image. The woman and I wondered whether the blackbird might be dead or injured. We watched it not move until the woman had to leave. After she had left, I went back out into the garden to look at the blackbird. It remained static at first but after a few seconds lifted its head and flew away. I was relieved. I had felt frightened at the idea that the blackbird would remain still, broken forever at the end of my garden.

I think the blackbird is our relationship, broken forever in my inbox, and it's time it flew away.

If you won't continue therapy with me through August then I'd like you to send me your final invoice and for this to be our last session.

Scarlett

13/08/1997

Good morning Scarlett,

I think it is difficult for you to feel that I am here to receive and contain your feelings when you cannot see or hear me. Perhaps this feeling was also present, to a lesser degree, when we were having sessions in-person. I'm reminded that, according to myth, a vampire's reflection cannot be seen in the mirror, so perhaps even in the consulting room you feared that there is only your reflection looking back at you, only yourself to talk to.

With that in mind, I understand that you find the thought of the upcoming break difficult but I don't think ending the therapy is the solution to that difficulty. Further, I am concerned that it may be damaging for you to end the therapy abruptly, especially when your mother is ill and you have little or no emotional support in DC.

However, if you decide you do want to end the therapy then I suggest that we perhaps have one or two sessions in September, after the break, by phone and work towards an ending 4-5 weeks from then, to give you time to process your feelings about the end of therapy and to think about what you want to take with you from it.

Best wishes,
Hannah

14/08/1997

Hannah,

'Perhaps' (that seems to be your favourite word!) I'd prefer talking to myself in the mirror than talking to you and having you make me feel worse. At least I'd know my reflection would be there and wouldn't decide to take a break at the last minute.

As I told you before I left for DC, it's not possible to have sessions by phone as 3pm UK time is 10am DC time and at that time on Tuesdays I'm always in the archive with no access to a landline, and I don't have a mobile phone.

I have thought about it carefully and decided that, if you insist on taking a break when I most need you, you are not the right therapist for me. I definitely want to end the therapy now so please send me your final invoice and I assume you will not be charging me for this E-mail as though it were a session.

Goodbye.

Scarlett

15/08/1997

Dear Scarlett,

I am sorry you feel that way but I accept and respect your decision. Should you wish to come back to therapy with me in the future, please contact me on my usual phone number. My door remains open to you.

I attach the final invoice, as requested, and wish you all the best for the future.

Kind wishes,
Hannah

Part II:
Unread Emails
1998 – 2009

There is no archive without a place of consignation, without a technique of repetition, and without a certain exteriority. No archive without outside.

Jacques Derrida, *Archive Fever* (1995)

28/11/1998

Hello Hannah,

I'm sure I'm breaching some sort of boundary by writing to you without permission but you did say that this E-mail account was set up especially for me, so maybe it continues to be mine to write to indefinitely. Perhaps you won't even know I've sent this message.

You might remember that I had originally gone to Washington DC to research the relationship between mothering and schizophrenia in Mead and Bateson's Balinese work and, as you could probably tell from the E-mail correspondence we had while I was there, the archive kind of took me over and I strayed a long way from what I had set out to do there. I let myself be guided, or perhaps misguided, by Derrida's writing on the archive and went down something of a rabbit hole. I'm not sure it has brought me to Wonderland though. I feel lost, Hannah. Lost, sad and stripped bare. I don't know what to think or where to turn to. I bet your patients say things like that to you all the time. Anyway, I'm not your patient any more, and I'm sad about that too, particularly the abrupt way it ended.

My funding for the project ran out last year and all I have to show for my time in DC is my own micro-archive of meticulously ordered digital photographs and my E-mails to you. I'm in an archival pit. Fran got together with someone new while I was away and my mother is very weak, thin and pained. She seems so far from herself, and even further from me. It can't be long now before she is completely gone.

Anyway, that's not why I'm writing to you. I'm writing to you because I'm stuck. The project feels dead but when I was in DC and writing to you, as difficult as that time was, it felt alive. I'm hoping that by writing to you again my ideas will be revitalised, that this E-mail address will bring me good luck, like a digital talisman.

So I'm going to tell you a little of what I'm thinking about Mead's archive at the moment. What I've become preoccupied with recently is the way in which Mead's oeuvre did not become what she'd hoped it would, that it was publicly debunked shortly after her death, and that she would have been aware of this debunking as she was dying in 1978 from pancreatic cancer. I imagine you would say I'm preoccupied with this because my mother is also at this end stage of life, dying from cancer, and I have some anxiety about whether my memories of her could be 'debunked', or sort of undone at the last minute. I often imagine what you would say, but then I go on and do what I would have done anyway. I'm not sure that's how therapy is supposed to work.

Anyway, back to Mead's posthumous debunking: You might know that despite Mead's rigorous methodologies, she is posthumously thought of as a popular national figure whose work is rarely taken seriously within the field of academic anthropology. This is in part due to the major criticism of Mead's work that emerged after her death. The criticism, or debunking, of her work concerned her first book, *Coming of Age in Samoa* (1928), in which, drawing on Freudian ideas around sexual repression and psychic development, Mead argues that in sexually liberated Samoan culture, adolescence is not experienced as a time of stress as it is in Western culture and, by extension, that there should be a freer attitude towards sexuality in American culture. The posthumous criticism came in the form of Derek Freeman's 1983 book *Margaret Mead and Samoa: The Making and Unmaking of an Anthropological Myth*, followed, in 1998, by his *The Fateful Hoaxing of Margaret Mead: A Historical Analysis of her Samoan Research*. Both books convincingly debunk Mead's Samoan research providing an empirical onslaught of counter-evidence on the basis of Freeman's archival research and own, more extensive, fieldwork in the area.

According to Freeman, Mead ignored a swathe of evidence that didn't support her conclusions, didn't adequately cross-reference or cross-check her data, and was hoaxed by two young girls, her main informants, who concocted tales of sexual promiscuity to delight the foreign visitor. So prolific was Mead as a popular anthropologist and (perhaps more notably) as a national figure, nicknamed 'mother' and sometimes 'grandmother to the world', that although he was a relatively unknown anthropologist at the time, Freeman's claims made national news. At first, he was ostracized by the anthropological community for criticizing its recently deceased figurehead, but as time went on the evidence against Mead's original findings gained credence, and the scientific veracity of Mead's work was irrevocably thrown into question, the Balinese research included.

Although some new ethnographic insights were noted by others shortly after it was shot, the posthumous reception of Mead's Balinese work was not what she had hoped for. In the main, it has been accessed for biographical rather than ethnographic purposes and so, contra her intentions, is taken to say more about Mead than it does the Balinese. She, rather than they, have become the object of study. The undoing of her archive and ethnographic standing by Freeman didn't happen officially until after her death, but Mead most likely saw it coming. In the mid 1970s, Freeman visited Mead while writing his book about how she was duped by her informants during her Samoan research and told her of his findings, of the fateful hoaxing on which her career was premised, making Mead aware of the future history of her debunking.

That's all for now. Thanks for reading it (assuming you've read this far...).

Scarlett

19/02/1999

Hi Hannah,

Well three months have passed and you haven't replied. It seems the digital talisman hasn't worked; I'm still lost in my writing and in my life, and I've no idea what to do with my seemingly inconsequential archive of my time in Mead's archive. Worst of all, my mum died last month. I don't know what to do about her archive either, by which I mean her house and everything in it. I've left it untouched, a dusty monument to a bohemian life, but it gives no comfort. The moment she died the house went cold and grey and no amount of lighting her candles or playing her music seems to change that. A bit like this E-mail address; my mother's house seems to have lost its magic since it was vacated by its owner.

Maybe something similar happened with Mead - all the physical records she busily made, the films, photographs, notes and so on, could not keep alive the Balinese people she went to study, instead they seem to have rendered them ghostly. Perhaps this haunting was the result of what Derrida calls archive fever, something from which I may also be suffering at present.

In addition to the debunking of her Samoan research, Mead's Balinese archive did not become the point of ethnographic reference that she had envisaged. Rather than accurately depicting the Balinese people, Mead's proliferating use of recording technologies seemed to reproduce them as ghosts.

The small amount of words published from the huge amount of written, photographic and filmic data from the field, might be understood as a fateful haunting that preceded her fateful hoaxing. In Bali, Mead's use of recording technology grew to an unprecedented scale. In a letter sent to Franz Boas, the mentor of her mentor, friend, and lover, Ruth Benedict, Mead wrote; 'I know you think I go into the field too much in proportion to writing up...' (April 1936) and perhaps in part a response to Boas's criticism, she continues; 'Where before I occasionally made a sample of behaviour over time which would run to two typewritten pages for an hour, we now have records of 15 typewritten pages and 200 feet of Ciné and a couple of hundred Leica stills for the same period. The recording is so much finer that I feel as if I were working at different levels from any work I've done previously' (April 1936).

Throughout her letters from Bali, Mead makes reference to her detailed and proliferating production of fieldnotes, photographs, models and film footage. In another letter to Boas on 28th August 1936 Mead writes '...we had ten days of meticulous recording of any tool change, sneeze, spit, wriggle, or exclamation by any one of the three [Balinese artists from Bedoeloe]...' She continues: 'When they finally went home we breathed a huge sigh of relief, but *we have had their ghosts with us practically ever since* as batches of the Leica prints or the Ciné films have come back from Batavia or....I have finished up another page of three columns of synchronised accounts' *(my italics)*. Mead, it seems, was haunted by the ghosts of her informants as they were channelled through recording technology, through the very technology with which she meticulously sought to capture them alive. In her descriptions of her endless films, photographs and fieldnotes, Bali and the Balinese exist as palimpsests, as shadowy phantoms of their tangible selves like 'the women carrying sheaves high on their heads so that in the dark they seem like prodigious masked figures'. (August 1936). There is an undercurrent of frustration, of an inability to sufficiently grasp the Balinese people who would seem to fade into ghosts the instant they were caught in the frame of her camera or stamped in the ink of her typewriter.

In response, it seems, Mead developed acutely detailed systems of classification, which could be seen as obsessional. In a letter sent on 13th May 1938, shortly after she had left Bali and arrived in Papua New Guinea, Mead relates the way in which she taxonomised even her own belongings and devised a hierarchical categorical system of who should inherit them: 'All the things we were going to leave behind us were sorted into grades of desirability, and we made lists of deservingness among the Bajoengese....I spread out all the middle-rate things in the dining room and permitted the mothers of much photographed children to make first choice in order of the amount of photography to which they had been subjected rather than the number of children. Each one went in and hesitated among the pillows, lamps, clothes, glass jars, etc.'

Mead's archive fever was something of a vicious circle; an attempt to control through repetitive recording and classifying the very haunting, or making dead, her records and systems of classification seemed to produce. I think these proliferating E-mails to you might be something of a vicious circle too; records of my struggles sent to someone who won't reply to them, which causes me to struggle further.

Scarlett

18/07/1999

Hi Hannah,

Do you remember that the avant-garde filmmaker, Maya Deren, unexpectedly showed up in the Margaret Mead collection? Well now she is turning up in my dreams. My mystery woman has been gradually transforming, which isn't unusual in itself, she often did shift her appearance, as you know. But I realised last night that she has become fixed in the form of Maya Deren, and I'm trying to work out what that means.

When I was in DC I discovered that Deren had not, in fact, shot part of the Balinese footage as the cataloguing notes implied. What the notes gave a clue to though, is Deren's request to view Mead and Bateson's Balinese footage in 1946, and the rather unexpected series of events that followed. I discovered, by locating in the archive the box of letters between them, that this avant-garde filmmaker played a larger part in the lives of Mead and Bateson than I could ever had imagined.

The story told by the letters in box K56 goes that Deren met Mead and Bateson at their house in New York on a Saturday night in December 1946. She followed up this social encounter with a long letter to Bateson in which she asks his forgiveness for 'keeping you both so late the other evening'. She asks for his feedback on an article she has written, which was inspired by a lecture Bateson gave on game theory at the New School. Evidently keenly aware of the differences between the field of anthropology and her own, she writes 'I hope you realize that the emphasis upon form, which may seem to you, in your field, superfluous, is on the contrary tremendously necessary in the contemporary art field, where a work of art is thought to be a personal finger painting of some kind'. Only four days later, Bateson responds with interest and enthusiasm for Deren's work, though warns against the difficulties of comparing two very different sets of ethnographic data - Haitian and Balinese - in the 'cross-cultural fugue' Deren has proposed, instead suggesting she compares Haitian material with that of another 'negro culture in the Caribbean'. Despite this, Deren persists in her wish to view and make use of Mead and Bateson's Balinese footage and borrows some portions of it. She was most drawn to Jane Belo's slow-motion footage, notably the most affecting, or 'artistic', in the Collection, which she would later mimic in the footage she shot of trance in Haiti. But that is not the only part of Belo's behaviour that she would unwittingly repeat; as Belo did during Mead and Bateson's time in Bali, Deren became Bateson's informal protégée and his lover.

Mead and Bateson's open relationship had seemed so far unshaken by both parties having extra-marital sexual encounters, but the word on the aisles of the Manuscript Reading Room at the Library of Congress was that it could not withstand Bateson's relationship with Deren, which began in 1946 and resulted in him leaving Mead in 1947, followed by their divorce in 1951. Mead was, by all accounts, distraught about the split. Unlike her two previous divorces, this one was not initiated by her and, reportedly, she remained in love with Bateson for the rest of her life.

But the relationship between Deren and Bateson was no fairy tale. During her relationship with Bateson, in 1947, Deren gained a Guggenheim Foundation Fellowship for 'creative work in the field of motion picture' to support her going to Haiti and making a film about trance and schizophrenia, and Bateson had planned to go with her. Reportedly Bateson ended the relationship with Deren just before their departure date in 1947 and Deren went to Haiti heartbroken.

Despite Deren's relationship with Bateson beginning and ending, her communication with Mead continues. Through a series of somewhat standoffish letters between them, in 1948 Deren and Mead strike up a deal about the Balinese footage Deren has borrowed. In exchange for the footage, which she has not returned, Deren agrees to give a portion of her Haitian footage to Mead's archive, to be held at the Institute for Intercultural Studies (which was run by Mead and later her daughter).

Deren asks for the money to cover the copies of the films in advance, Mead obliges and sends her a cheque for $662.50, for which she demands a receipt. In 1949, Deren has run out of money to finish her Haitian project and applies for another Guggenheim fellowship for which she asks Mead to be the referee. Mead agrees but sends the reference too late and Deren is unsuccessful in her application. In 1951 the Haitian prints, for which Deren has been paid in advance, still have not arrived at the Museum, and Mead has become 'very uneasy' about their whereabouts. Deren's response does not allay her anxieties - she says the prints may be at the back of her closet but seems in no rush to locate them. Deren says she will work on locating the 'Museum stuff' once she has finished her book on Haiti *(Divine Horseman)* and 'collapsed for at least 2 weeks (minimum estimate!)'. As if this weren't enough of a put-down of the famed anthropologist, Deren ends the letter by twisting the knife and asking Mead for Bateson's new address.

I can't help being pleased about Deren's audacity, her refusal to bow to Mead, and I find something comforting, though incestuous, about her plump feline lips and onyx curls strutting across the grounds of my unconscious. Now she is my mystery woman I've been drawn into the archive, as if I'm an active player in this raunchy 1940s New York art scene. Maybe Deren allows me to collude with her against Mead, to let her be my bad object of study. I can't seem to make Mead good so perhaps it is easier, instead, to bring her down.

Scarlett

20/03/2000

Hi Hannah,

Well I don't think it's the effect of the digital talisman but somehow it seems the magic is back and I'm able to write. Maybe it's because at least one good thing, an important thing, has happened in my life recently, or perhaps it's the effect of having entered the twenty-first century, that I have managed to get a perspective on the archive from which I am able to think.

In this last year, since my mother's death, it is as though my life, like hers remembered, has entered a state of temporal anarchy. Different times come crashing in on me in an unexpected and often unwanted fashion. Sometimes I wake up sure that I'm living in the house I moved out of five years ago, with the wrong partner in bed next to me, or that I'm nine years old and lying under the eaves in my bedroom at 21 Abingdon Road, waiting for my mother to tell me to get up and ready for school. I often wake in the night believing I'm a small child and sleeping-over at a friend's house, and I long for my mother to come to collect me and take me home. Life-times that had been vague memories are now fleetingly tangible and present, along with the previously inaccessible emotional and sensory details that go with them. It's as though the memories previously held for me by my mother, who guarded my life history for me in her house-archive and in her memory, have been unleashed and are flying back at me.

I'm attaching the first proper piece of writing I've been able to produce since I returned from DC. It's not a long chapter by academic standards, but it is a chapter, and one that, for now at least, I will allow nobody but you to read. When you do you will hopefully understand why *Archive Fever* has such resonance for me, and why I thought you would like it. I've been thinking about what you asked me in DC, about 'Derridaddy', as I now like to call him, and what it is I feel I can't say about the archive in my own voice, or my own name. I think I'm starting to prize that question open, to push back at him, and to process my experience in DC and the grief and confusion I feel since my mother's death. I've also included my child self in the text, but in the third person. I know you don't approve of my third-person games, but I hope you will understand why I need to play them at the moment.

Scarlett

Umbilical Cord

> We must come to the moment at which Yerushalmi seems to suspend everything, in particular everything he has said and done up to this point, from the thread of a discreet sentence. One could be tempted to regard this thread as the umbilical cord of the book. Everything seems to be suspended from this umbilical cord—by the umbilical cord of the event which such a book as this represents. For in a work entirely devoted to memory and to archive, a sentence on the last page says the future.
>
> Jacques Derrida, *Archive Fever* (1995)

Since the early 1990s the 'archive' has become of central concern to a range of disciples including anthropology, philosophy, history, comparative literature and political science and, as a result, has generated a large collection, one might say 'archive', of literature consisting of conflicting views on its form, function and meaning. It was mainly as a result of the works of postmodern writers, in particular Derrida and Foucault, that the archive has been thrown into question in this way, transformed from a being regarded purely as a 'source' to a subject of study in its own right. For Foucault, the archive is not merely 'the sum of all the texts that a culture has kept upon its person attesting to its own past' (1972:128) but a system of discursivity that determines the limits of what can be said, and upon which entities such as disciplines, institutions and states define their own truth criteria. Following Foucault, for the founder of postcolonial studies, Edward Said, the archive is a knowledge producing apparatus, encompassing museums, libraries, literature, law, and more, and was the foundation on which the British Empire was built. For others, the archive is as broadly defined but less connected with knowledge and power than with questions of technology, indeed for many social and cultural theorists the world wide web is a giant virtual archive and the archive is constituted by all digital and as well as all material culture.

The Structure of the Archive

Derrida's *Archive Fever* (1995) is of particular relevance to my empirically-based and materially concerned research because the book is so embroiled with its particular archive, or object of research—with one historian's (Yerushalmi's) rendering of Freudian psychoanalysis—that it breaks down the distinction between theoretical framework and the subject to which it is applied. For Derrida, the Freudian archive is both the subject of *Archive Fever* and the model through which 'archive fever' [*mal d'archive*], the phenomenon, can come into being. Following a *Note, Exergue, Preamble,* and

Foreword amounting to eighty-two pages, the thirteen-page *Theses* begins. The book, originally written to be read aloud as a lecture given at the Freud Museum in London, makes evident that the archival 'drive', its inextricable binding to the death drive, and the resulting 'fever' or malaise, can only be understood in the terms of Freud's lexicon, in the terms of the archive, or corpus of work (the body of psychoanalysis), to which it is applied and from which it emerged.

An engagement with the material details, or tactility, of a particular archive is not present in Derrida's framework but neither is it necessarily precluded. Although not attentive to the material form of the documents within the archive, Derrida is very attentive to technologies of archiving which, for him, encompass all recording and communications technologies, email in particular. In *Archive Fever*, Derrida argues that the writing, sending and receiving of letters by Freud, Jung and their colleagues, was necessary for the development of psychoanalysis, itself an archive. He emphasises that 'archivable meaning is always in advance co-determined by the structure that archives' (1995:18).

> Scarlett's bedroom was a large box with glass doors at the front and windows at the back, placed onto the flat roof of their house. It could be found, bright and solitary, at the top of the second, and final, flight of stairs. From the street the room appeared an incongruous appendage, sitting modern, flat-rooved and uncomfortable amidst a jumble of eighteenth and

nineteenth century, pointed rooftops. Outside the glass doors to the front of the bedroom-box was a white-tiled roof terrace that overlooked the small urban street below. On summer nights, after Scarlett had been put to bed, her mother would creep through her bedroom and out of these doors to water the large pot-plants that flanked the roof terrace. There would be the sound of the bolts clonking open, top and bottom, the unsteady clicks of the brass keys turning in their wobbly locks, then an interlude of noise and odour from the pubs at either end of Abingdon Road. The drunken voices, explosions of laughter and wafts of industrial toilet cleaner and deep-fryer fat bounced their way up the front of the small houses on the narrow street and into Scarlett's bedroom. They made a strange lullaby, but one that she found comforting.

The force of the archive's codetermining structure is evident in the Margaret Mead Papers and South Pacific Ethnographic Archives held at the Library of Congress. Mead catalogued the vast amount of photographs, notes and films she and Bateson produced in Bali in 1936-8, with such an intricate system of cross-referencing that the body of data could be said to be born an archive. To quote Mead's diary, 'with this kind of record even thirty years later I can place each moment or write captions that include the identification of a child's foot in the corner of a picture'. There is, however, a split between the way Mead imagined her archive would be held and the way it is ordered at the Library of Congress. Mead's multi-media archive relies on a system of cross-referencing between film, photographs and film cataloguing notes. In order to cross-reference the films, photographs and notes from the Balinese material, as Mead intended, to tell the exact time, location and individual in a sequence of events down to the identification of a foot in the corner of a picture, you would need to have all three media present at once. But the 'technical structure of the archiving archive' (to borrow Derrida's phrasing) at the Library of Congress does not allow for this. The Manuscript Reading Room, where Mead's written archive is kept, is a five-minute journey down a series of warren-like tunnels and up two service elevators away from the Motion Picture Division where her films are stored. A few photographs are kept in the Manuscript Reading Room but the majority are in yet another (photographic) division of the Library. Because it is impossible to have the notes, films and photographs together in the same room (they are all reference only so cannot be taken out of their different respective locations), one cannot use the archive in the way Mead intended. "Piffle!" A favourite expression of hers, is what I imagine she would say to that.

Like the anthropologist arriving in a foreign land, the researcher arriving in the archive is a lonely and disorientating experience. The archive, as a physical space, is an unfamiliar and sometimes unmapped terrain that operates with its own particular laws, customs and rituals which one must learn and agree to abide by. This can often be challenging, and the odd faux pas will inevitably be made by the visitor to the unfamiliar place. Like the modernist anthropologist, the researcher in the archive is also likely to experience shock, boredom, loneliness, fascination, confusion, and repetitive strain injury. These various experiences of archival research are perhaps enhanced when the archive is also in a foreign land, as with my experience at the Library of Congress.

> Scarlett and her mother's house was a small eighteenth century cottage fronting right onto the street. To the left, their house adjoined one identical cottage, and to the right a mish-mash of shops, B&Bs and halfway houses which ran off the Earls Court Road in what was one of the most eclectic and transient areas of London. Scarlett's mother proudly labelled the neighbourhood, usually after relaying a story from her morning chat with 'the nice boys at the gay brothel', or giving directions to some Australians from the local backpackers, 'the dregs of the Royal Borough' (of Kensington and Chelsea, that is).

But the experience of the researcher is not the only connection between ethnography and the archive. The archival drive to collect, preserve, and maintain, or to return to an imagined birth place, which is threatened and constituted by the competing death drive in Derrida's account, could be understood to have motivated all of modernist anthropology, which laboured under the idea that it was preserving humanity in its primitive state before irreversible changes would be brought about, in particular by the Second World War in the case of Mead's attempts to 'preserve' traditional Balinese life through photography and film in the late 1930s. This nostalgic sentiment is echoed at the end of the classic ethnography *Tristes Tropiques* (1955) by Claude Lévi-Strauss, whose structuralist writing was influenced by Freud and foundational to the poststructuralist writing of Derrida. Lévi-Strauss laments the loss that he believes will be brought about by 'civilization' producing 'what physicists call entropy . . . that is inertia'. He continues that 'every verbal exchange, every printed line, establishes communication between people, thus creating an evenness of level, where before there was an information gap and consequently a greater degree of organization' (1955/1977:413-4). Lévi-Strauss pre-emptively goes on to exclaim 'Oh! fond farewell to savages and explorations!' Ironically, and congruent with the etymology of Lévi-Strauss's neologism 'entropology', which he argues could be a new term to describe anthropology, the threat of this inertia is what makes the Other enticingly other. Like the archive, it appears that otherness itself is inscribed with its own undoing; that its attraction is constituted by its imminent disappearance is an inherent death drive.

It seems that the archive's silent insistence that one must document, record, preserve, is stronger than the materials that are produced as a result. Put cynically, not only do archival documents decay (analogue) or fall subject to viruses and corruption (digital), but they do not fulfil the promise of reproduction of live-events even when they are intact. Despite this, and the fact that archives are notoriously under-accessed, there seems to be a public consensus that archives must remain. The desire for archives to be kept, though rarely used, suggests that they function as tools of forgetting rather than tools of remembering; archives hold the past so that we don't have to. The archive's containing of the past (the temporal other) might be akin to modernist anthropology's containing of the primitive (the cultural other), through ethnographic explanation, order and supposedly scientific classification. It can also be linked to the motive of most home movies: parents' desire to preserve their children in a state of youth and purity before the inevitable happens and they grow into unruly teens or disappointing adults.

In the Mead Collection are vast amounts of footage of her and Bateson's only child, Mary Catherine Bateson, who, it has been said, was the most filmed child in America at the time. The photographic and, I would argue, filmic recording of children, like that of 'primitives', fulfils a nostalgic desire to return to a birth place, to follow an imaginary umbilical cord. Might the homesickness or sentimentality that drives parents to record their children, and the modernist anthropologist to record the primitive, be symptomatic of the archival drive? This archival drive could not be in play without the presence of the death drive, which is intrinsic to archive fever. As Derrida reminds us: 'there would be no archival desire without the radical finitude, without the possibility of a forgetfulness which does not limit itself to repression. Above all, and this is the most serious, there is no archive fever without the threat of this death drive, this aggression and destructive drive' (1995:19).

The Uncanny

If Derrida is right, it is no surprise that ethnography, home movies, and the archive proper all wield something of the uncanny. In his essay *The Uncanny* (1919) Freud argues that the unconscious mind has an instinctual compulsion to repeat, and that whatever reminds us of this compulsion is perceived as uncanny (1919:238). For Freud, uncanny feeling can also be aroused when there is uncertainty as to whether an object is alive or not, the distinction between reality and the imaginary is effaced, or when a symbol takes on the full function of the thing it symbolises. The essay *The Uncanny* is uncanny in itself (and therefore yet more uncanny because it takes on the full function of the thing it symbolises) because it eerily avoids naming the death drive, although it would seem that this is what Freud describes throughout. It was not until a year later in *Beyond the Pleasure Principle* (1920) that Freud first named the death drive (sometimes translated as the 'death instinct') which he describes as having a 'regressive character' on the basis of 'the facts of the compulsion to repeat' (1920/1984:338). On the same page, Freud tentatively comes to the conclusion that '[t]he pleasure principle seems actually to serve the death drive', and this is mirrored by Derrida's argument that archival desire seems actually to serve the 'anarchivic', 'archiviolithic' death drive.

> In the summer, people would sit on their windowsill eating takeaway meals of fish 'n' chips, Chinese, Indian or Filipino food, all of which were available in the nearby streets. The outside-in windowsill allowed Scarlett to hear the conversations of adult strangers as if they were in the room with her, or she were on the windowsill with them. Later, perhaps as a result of the unprotecting structures in which she was raised, Scarlett would keep slipping over and skidding off what seemed to her a rather feeble boundary between private and public, inside and outside, home and away, self and other.

Ethnography in particular, and home movie-making to an extent, are also uncanny because of their mingling of the familiar and the strange, of their 'inside-and-outside-ness' or 'unhomeliness'. Freud thinks beyond Jentsch's prior definition of the uncanny as being synonymous with the unfamiliar, stating that 'among its different shades of meaning the word *'heimlich'* [homely] exhibits one which is identical to its opposite *'unheimlich'* [uncanny]' (Freud 1919:224). *Heimlich* [homely] refers both to what is agreeable and familiar and to what is concealed and kept out of sight—everything is *unheimlich* [unhomely/uncanny] that ought to have remained secret and hidden but has come to light (1919:225). There is something comforting, or homely, in the consignation of visual relics from the past into the shadows of an archive. Their resurrection, or bringing to light, is marked, however, by something uneasy or unhomely.

The uncanny, then, arises contextually, often through an inversion of binaries, a kind of turning inside-out where matter becomes eerily out of place. Perhaps nowhere is this better demonstrated than between the related projects of surrealism, ethnography, and psychoanalysis during the inter-war period and their inverted play on the familiar and the strange. All three endeavours were interested in the idea of the Other, the primitive Other in particular, but more centrally in the unconscious; of the ethnographic other/primitive (ethnography), of the individual/self (psychoanalysis) and of capitalist culture (surrealism). As a result of their focus on the unconscious, both surrealism and ethnography were undoubtedly hugely influenced by psychoanalysis, indeed Mead and her long-term lover, Ruth Benedict, reportedly gave each other psychoanalysis in the early days of their relationship, engaging in sessions where they took it in turns to play the role of analyst and analysand.

It might be said that the mixing of anthropology, surrealism and psychoanalysis is a distinctly modernist version of interdisciplinarity. All three sought to bring to light something of unconscious processes but to different ends and with different relationships to the uncanny effects this uncovering might produce. While surrealism actively accentuated the uncanny aspects of unconscious recovery for political purposes through the interplay of the familiar and the strange, modernist anthropology sought to dissipate the uncanny qualities of the primitive by fixing it within a safe, scientific paradigm. Similarly, psychoanalysis was keen to prove its scientific worth in the face of criticism that its methods were imprecise, not open to proof by experiment, that it was unscientific, or a 'Jewish Science'. Like Freud's psychoanalysis, Mead's ethnographic work sought, implicitly, to separate itself from surrealism, framing the former as science versus the latter as art, a border she keenly policed. And it was the case that from the 1930s onwards, anthropology and psychoanalysis sat more comfortably together as 'sciences', with the art of surrealism becoming something of the black sheep of this family of three. We might wonder how the disciplines of anthropology and psychoanalysis could have evolved differently, perhaps more richly, if the surreal, or 'artistic' elements of their endeavours had been embraced at this point in history, rather than repressed.

> Like Scarlett and her mother's house, the house next door had low ceilings and little light. Scarlett remembers going there only once, but she remembers it well. Their next-door neighbours were a gay couple called Howard and Geoffrey. Scarlett's mother told her that she would especially like Geoffrey because, like her, he wrote poetry. Indeed, it did greatly appeal to Scarlett, at eight years old, to meet a real, adult poet. It also appealed to Scarlett to go into a house, the only house, that looked like theirs from the outside. She imagined that seeing other people living in a mirrored abode might make her domestic space seem more regular, more

connected with other interiors than with the unruly outside. In some ways it did. Scarlett was impressed with Howard and Geoffrey's cosy, traditional furniture, particularly their soft paisley-patterned armchair and tall, pink, tasselled lamp.

Despite what might be understood as the shunning of surrealism by both anthropology and psychoanalysis, this art perhaps offered a key to the unconscious that anthropology hoped to unlock by ethnographic means, and psychoanalysis by clinical means. In turn, psychoanalysis offered surrealism a foundation on which to develop an art, and a theory, of unconscious associations and desires, indeed it may well have been the case that surrealism could not have developed without the advent of psychoanalysis. A closer relationship between surrealism and psychoanalysis was sought when André Breton, who was arguably as foundational to surrealism as Freud was to psychoanalysis, first wrote to Freud in 1919, and visited him in 1921. Despite their shared interests in the primitive and uncovering unconscious processes, Freud was less than enthusiastic about Breton's surrealist project. To one of Breton's flattering letters about the importance of psychoanalysis to the surrealist movement, Freud replied 'I'm afraid it is unclear to me what surrealism is and what it wants', or, in German, *Was Will das Weib* (Freud quoted in Jones 1974:468). Curiously, this line echoes Freud's famous words in a letter he wrote to Marie Bonaparte in which he asks 'what does a woman want' which, in German, is also *Was Will das Weib*, mirroring exactly the line he wrote to Breton about surrealism.

Although Freud and psychoanalysis did not come to embrace Breton and surrealism as they might have (and one might wonder what alternative direction psychoanalysis may have taken if it had), they perhaps shared more than Freud cared to admit. Not only did they have a similar attitude towards the psyche, but also towards women, by whom they appeared equally perplexed. Echoing Freud's question 'what does a woman want', Breton took the view that women are 'the most marvellous and disturbing question in all the world'. It is this jointly held bafflement about women stemming, perhaps, from a denial of women's resistance to accepting their place within a patriarchal structure, that has lead feminist thinkers and writers to either shun or attempt to recalibrate psychoanalytic and surrealist canons. In her book *What Does a Woman Want*, Shoshana Felman asks, in relation to the title question, 'Is it in the power of this question to engender, through the literary or the psychoanalytic work, a woman's voice as its speaking subject' (1993:3). Angela Carter is less hopeful about the surrealists. In her 1975 essay "The Alchemy of the Word" she writes 'The Surrealists were not good with women. That is why, although I thought they were wonderful, I had to give them up in the end.'

A Feminist Incision

So, what does this mean for Derrida, a self-proclaimed feminist, and his poststructuralist approach to Freud's archive and Yerushalmi's rendering of it? *Archive Fever*, while it acknowledges patriarchy, is certainly not a feminist text; it does not open up the possibility for the archive to be other than patriarchal, not consciously at least. However, there is a particular moment in Derrida's densely woven corpus on the 'patriarchal' archive, quoted in this chapter's opening epigraph, where an alternative reading might be opened up and a feminist incision might be made. I use the word 'incision' with intent, for we enter at the point of Freud's circumcision, where and when, approximately seven days after his birth, 'the archive marked once in his body' (Derrida 1995:41). The incision is an uncanny one if, according to Freud, we approach it from the outside. Derrida quotes Freud's description of 'the *impression* which circumcision leaves on those who are uncircumcised: "a disagreeable uncanny [*unheimlich*] impression"' (1995:46). To those for whom it is unfamiliar, circumcision is uncanny, not only because it is unfamiliar or that it arouses castration anxiety, but also because of the interplay of familiarity and unfamiliarity, because the circumcised individual can be felt to be an uncanny double of the uncircumcised.

> Geoffrey took Scarlett onto his knee, the armchair embracing them both, and read her one of his poems. It was about a Robin Redbreast, a bird that Scarlett had always found particularly comforting. Scarlett can't remember much about the poem now, but for her feeling as Geoffrey read, that there was more in the words than she could understand. For a

year or more after the visit, Scarlett felt comforted by the cosy next-door house with its warm armchair, pink lamp and Robin Redbreast poem. She imagined that her home and theirs were each half of the same lovingly made inkblot. Like a mirrored twin, or a next of kin, the house next-door was somewhere Scarlett would know in her sleep.

Derrida's interest in the event of Freud's circumcision, however, is not only about its relationship to the uncanny feelings it may arouse for the uncircumcised. Rather, it is in relation to Yerushalmi's referring to Freud as 'we', more specifically as 'we Jews' who have, he says, in the question of whether or not psychoanalysis is a Jewish science, an equal stake (1995:41). Yerushalmi's book *Freud's Moses: Judaism Terminable and Interminable* (1991) is, for Derrida, retrospectively determined by its final section entitled *Monologue with Freud*, in which Yerushalmi switches from referring to Freud in third person, to referring to him in the second. Derrida argues that Yerushalmi's 'we' is a covenant to which Freud can only say 'yes', as with the covenant that he entered as a baby at the moment of his circumcision—*'"I shall say 'we'"*—when it is addressed to a phantom or newborn' (1995:41), writes Derrida of Yerushalmi's addressing of Freud. It is not only the case that Yerushalmi ventiloquises Freud, or re-circumcises him, but that in being called to witness as a second person, Freud, or Freud's ghost as channelled through Yerushalmi, must respond. What is significant here is the attention paid, not to the archive as law, power, and knowledge (although this is also important to Derrida's thought on the archive), but to the specificity of 'the historian's object become spectral subject' (1995:39).

Threading this back to our point of entry, it is in Yerushamli's *Monologue with Freud*, the final section of his book, in which he addresses Freud in the second person, forcing him to again enter a (Jewish) covenant as he did at his circumcision, that Derrida identifies as providing 'the umbilical cord opening of the future' (1995:40). The sentence of Yerushalmi's to which Derrida refers reads: 'Much will depend, of course, on how the very terms Jewish and science are to be defined' (1991:100). Yerushalmi's address to the future renders the present archival, and in so doing frames the archive as a ghostly relation operating within multiple tenses, rather than as a concept dealing exclusively with the past. For Derrida, this address written in the future tense, this knowledge suspended in the conditional, poses the archive as a question not of the past, but of the future. The umbilical cord of Yerushalmi's book is an appeal to the future, like an answer machine message waiting to be heard.

Given that Derrida poses the archive, like circumcision, as a paternally inscribed institution, it is curious that he describes the crux of Yerushalmi's book, and therefore the crux of his own book (namely that the archive is a question of the future), as an umbilical cord from which 'everything is suspended'. Why equate Yerushalmi's relationship with the dead arch-patriarch, and the (patriarchal) archive's relationship to the future, with the figure of the mother's body feeding her foetus? Perhaps the key to the maternal, or 'in utero', metaphor is in the 'suspension'. The expectant mother, like the expectant address to the future, is held in a state of suspension, or abeyance.

Curiously, given that all the clues are there, the archive as an expectant or abeyant site, as an abode (or *demeure* in French), is not attended to in *Archive Fever*. Instead, through an etymological discussion of the archive in the first few pages, the archive is framed as deriving from the home of the archons; a place of commencement and commandment. On the second page of *Archive Fever* Derrida follows the etymology of "archive" to the Greek *arkheion*. The *Arkheion* was 'initially a house, a domicile, an address, the residence of the superior magistrates, the *archons*, those who commanded' (1995:2). Derrida goes on to elucidate that these archons, these superior magistrates, were citizens who held political power and had the right to represent and to make the law. Because of this publicly recognized right, it was in their homes that official documents were filed, and it was they who had the right to guard and interpret the archives. While illuminating, this is not an exhaustive exploration of the archive's relation to place and containment, in my view, and overlooks what might be understood to be the maternal qualities of the archive.

The Maternal Archive

> One sunny morning, Scarlett's mother called her, beaming with disbelief, to come and look outside. In the middle of the road was the tall, pink, tassled lamp switched on, cord trailing into the house, and the paisley

armchair with Geoffrey nestled into it, reading. A handful of passing pedestrians had gathered to look at the scene with a mix of curiosity and concern. Scarlett's mother was brimming with laughter that communicated 'how wonderfully eccentric!' but for Scarlett this absurdity was far from funny. She found the scene frightening, and the brazen madness of a man on whose lap she had sat, a disturbing betrayal, but of what she could not be sure; of her sense of mirrored stability perhaps, or of her mother's duty to protect her. Within a week of this event, Geoffrey died in a car crash. He had been driving alone, on his way to a writing retreat, her mother said. She added that although Geoffrey had been driving only a little over the speed limit, he had been driving too fast for the conditions; it was raining and visibility was poor. His car spun out of control as he crossed into the fast lane. This image of a car spinning out of control in the rain, the instant of Geoffrey's death, made a deep impression on Scarlett and the once warm and comforting twin house became a disturbing reflection, a deathly double.

In 1998, three years after the publication of *Archive Fever*, *Derrida's Demeure: Fiction and Testimony*, a response to Maurice Blanchot's *The Instant of my Death* (1994) was published.

The book utilizes, not in the context of the archive but of (auto)biographical truthfulness, the multiple meanings springing from the root of the French noun *demeure*. The English translation of *demeure* proffered by Elizabeth Rottenberg in her translation of the text is 'the abode' which, in its various linguistic incarnations, might be a *prêt-a-porter* angle on the nuances of the archive; a notion that cannot do without residence, as Derrida puts it in *Archive Fever*. Derrida writes the following in reference to the distinction between autobiography and fiction in *Demeure*, but I think it could equally be a way of framing the archive:

> I will attempt to speak of this necessary but impossible abidance of the abode. How can one decide what remains abidingly. How is one to hear the term—the noun or the verb, the adverbial phrases—*"abode"*, "that which abides", "that which holds *abidingly*," "that by which one must *abide*"?
>
> (1998:16)

What I want to suggest is that the noun *abode* could be descriptive of Derrida's reading of the archive in the sense that it means 'a place of residence', as could the verb *abide* be used with and without object; to *abide* is to remain, dwell, continue in a particular condition, and to *abide [with object]* is to tolerate and endure, and to await, and of course one must abide by the laws of the archive, of archival consignation. Furthermore *abeyance*, in law, is an indeterminate state of ownership when, for example, after a death the person entitled to the deceased's estate has not been ascertained. This could also be said to describe the state archival documents are in prior to them being claimed by a researcher, historian or archivist who might bring them into the conscious, public domain. Furthermore, the root of the English translation (abode) of the French noun (*demeure*) is itself derivative of the middle French *abaer* meaning *to expect*. The point I want to make about the archive and the 'abode' is its two-fold relation to place or physical containment, and to expectancy. Firstly, it reiterates and reframes the necessity of, at least in the case of analogue archives, a physical place or 'home' for the archive. I say 'reiterate' as well as reframe because although Derrida does not discuss the abode (*demeure*) in *Archive Fever*, he is interested in the archive's domiciliation. In respect of its relationship to the historian's object rendered spectral, for example, he writes 'haunting implies places, a habitation, and always a haunted house' (1995:86). Derrida continues to describe the archival drive as a form of 'homesickness', a drive to return to a place of commencement and commandment (as with the house of the archons) which is threatened by a conflicting death drive which is 'above all *anarchivic*, one could say, or *archiviolithic* . . . [or] archive destroying' (1995:10).

> Years later, when Scarlett was in her teens, her mother told her, as she was now old enough, that she used to hear Geoffrey and Howard having sex on the other side of her bedroom wall, and that whenever Geoffrey climaxed would scream, in a strange high-pitched voice, "Mummy!". Mother said

that sometimes, in her half sleep, she had thought this cry came from Scarlett and had called back 'are you alright sweetie?' only to realise her mistake when no reply was given. Scarlett hoped her mother had made this up. She was both disappointed and relieved never to have heard the bizarre cry from the haunted house next door, nor her mother's mistaken response to it.

It is pertinent to note here, as Derrida does in *Archive Fever*, that some of Freud's papers, artefacts, and frozen final consulting room remain held at 20 Maresfield Gardens. Still very much resembling a grand family home, you can find the Freud Museum today nestled among other Hampstead mansions, a short walk from the Anna Freud Centre, and (as a Kleinian psychotherapist once put it to me) within 'spitting distance' of the Kleinian Tavistock Clinic. Despite its significance as part of the legacy of Freud, 20 Maresfield Gardens was in fact his home for only a very short time; from 1938 when he and Anna arrived after fleeing Nazi-occupied Vienna, until his death in September 1939.

The Freud Museum, the last home of Sigmund Freud, is perhaps a physical exemplar of the archive's relationship to memorialization, patriarchy and domiciliation, of its need for a haunted house. It is fitting, then, that it was at the Freud Museum that Derrida first presented *Archive Fever* as a lecture in June 1994 which, at the time, was entitled 'The Concept of the Archive: A Freudian Impression'. The Freudian archive, in keeping with Derrida's conceptualization of the archive, is announced as a paternal institution. But might the maternal qualities of the archive have been repressed in this theorization, only to re-emerge three years later in the form of the abode in Derrida's *Demeure: Fiction and Testimony* (1998)? Despite the Freudian archive's relationship to a literal house, an *abode*, and the relationship of the concept of the archive to the noun abode and its etymological link to expectancy, Derrida does not attend to, perhaps represses, the relationship between the archive and the maternal in *Archive Fever*. However, by describing Yerushalmi's climactic sentence as an umbilical cord Derrida makes a move, perhaps a slip, towards the maternal, by suspending the very future of the archive on a pregnant metaphor. It is this slip revealing the matriarchal qualities of the archive, this accidental pregnancy, that I feel compelled to follow.

15/11/2000

Hi Hannah,

I wonder whether you've read the chapter, or if you ever will. You might notice that I didn't include Maya Deren in it, despite the detail of her relationship with Mead and Bateson being quite a discovery in the history of their fields. It may not be maximising on my research in DC but I don't want to share what I know about Deren in the formal outputs of my research. I want to keep her to myself, let her relationship with Bateson and our dream-affair be my secret.

The inclusion of Deren in Mead's archive, and in my dreams, has got me thinking about Mead's relationship (or lack of a relationship) to art and the avant-garde but more specifically to the surrealism of the 1920s and 30s that was in its heyday when she embarked on her trip to Bali. I have developed a theory, again one just for you and not for publication, that she may have been a secret surrealist. If you've read the chapter you'll know that the 1930s was a time at which surrealism and ethnography were relatively intertwined, and Bali was known as an island residence for the avant-garde scene more than it was of formal ethnographic interest.

James Clifford, the main proponent of the 'Writing Culture' debate in anthropology during the 1980s, writes that every ethnographer is 'something of a surrealist, a reinventor and reshuffler of realities' (1988:147). This seems acutely true of Mead, especially when we look at her reappropriation of the dance I told you about at the end of our correspondence in DC, the one in which Mead and Bateson's 'sycophantic' informant, Rawa, is wounded by the *Kris* [dagger] that a real trance would have supposedly protected him from, and is then violently attacked by another of Mead's ethnographic subjects; the crazed Pemankoe.

In 1953, the film *Trance and Dance in Bali*, which was the main output of Mead and Bateson's Balinese research, was aired on national television in a CBS broadcast, with Mead being interviewed by presenter, Douglas Edwards. Mead tells the audience twice that these are 'real trances' with 'nothing corny about them'. Her confident voiceover to the film, which omits the bloody scene, informs us with absolute certainty when each of the participants goes in and out of trance, seems to confirm this. Douglas Edwards is not fully convinced, asking Mead, despite her reassurances, whether she can definitely tell who is really in trance. She continues, unwaveringly, in the affirmative. The archive, however, tells a different, or several different, stories. Although it is presented as a single event, *Trance and Dance in Bali* in fact combines footage from two different trance performances both from Pagoetan in lowland Bali; one relatively undramatic in 1939 and the other, the bloody *Kris* dance featuring Rawa and Pemankoe. Nonetheless, by Mead's own reckoning, which she announces in the voice over the *Trance and Dance in Bali*, a solid evidential indication of someone being in trance during the *kris* dance is that they will not be cut by the *krisses* as they appear to stab themselves.

A straight telling of the bloody goings on in the trance recorded in the archive would prove, according to Mead's own logic, that at least Rawa's trance was fake, yet footage of this 'trance' forms a major part of the film that supposedly contains 'nothing corny'. Furthermore, Mead frames the shot so that the western audience, whom we know from the notes were present, cannot be seen. Mead demanded that the performance took place, orchestrated its timing (that it took place in the morning when the light would be better rather than in the afternoon or evening as usual), chose which actors were to take part in it (more 'photogenic' women than men), and her presence may have been responsible for the violent outbreak during it, yet she claims it is objective with nothing corny. In Mead's Balinese research, then, it was not her informants, but she, who was responsible for a kind of surrealist reshuffling of reality, or hoaxing.

Despite the interesting 'teasers' in the archive, Mead's didactic voiceover in *Trance and Dance in Bali* reduces the violent events of Rawa and Pemankoe, among others, to a familiar, supposedly universal narrative; 'and so the Balinese re-enact the struggle between death on the one hand and life protecting ritual on the other' we are told in the concluding line of the film. One might say that the anthropologists' rendering of their experiences in Bali were more schizoid than the behaviour they set out to study; the surreal Bali of violence and confusion produced in the archive seems entirely split from the clean and ordered version of events in *Trance and Dance in Bali*. The published accounts of Mead's research neatly repress violence and uncertainty leaving a mass of contradictory and sometimes gruesome data in the archive, like a collection of muffled ghosts. I'm discovering that my agenda in this project is to uncover those parts of the archive that are deemed too messy or too bloody and left out of official accounts. I want to unmuffle the ghosts and allow them to speak freely.

Scarlett

08/06/2002

Hi Hannah,

When I said at the end of the Umbilical Cords chapter that I felt compelled to follow an accidental pregnancy, I didn't realise it was soon to have such resonance in my personal life. I'm going to leave that as a teaser for you...

Anyway, it's not only in my personal life - in my professional life there has also been a significant birth for me this year. While scanning the catalogues of a small regional film archive in Chichester, the Screen Archive South East (SASE), I discovered a new collection that was donated to the archive just a few weeks ago. The films were made by a Swedish diplomat called Theodor Wistrand who conducted an amateur ethnography of East and South East Asia in 1938-9. Very unusually for the time, he filmed mostly in colour and, as a result, the Wistrand Collection contains the earliest colour footage of Korea and of Bali.

The absence of colour in Mead's photographic and film recordings is a result of the commonly held view at the time that the sumptuousness of colour recording was inappropriate for scientific research and would render it somehow 'artistic'. Mead therefore avoided colour recording, seeing its absence as a marker of scientific rigour.

Wistrand's films, then, offer a curious counter-perspective to Mead's, a less formal but more accurate perspective, it might be argued. For example, Wistrand films a very similar *Kris* dance to that involving Rawa and Pemankoe, and his footage provides a colour-version of how a less considered angle of the 'authentic' dance might have looked: Brightly adorned Balinese onlookers chatting and laughing while Europeans in white hats and gloves perch along a small wall, their black motor cars lined up on the road behind as they wait for the touristic spectacle to begin.

But it's not only the comparison with Mead's footage that draws me to Wistrand's. His footage seems to speak to me directly; the way the rainbow recordings of his daughters, servants, day trips and kittens are muddled in with the unedited amateur ethnography reminds me of the home movies of my childhood and my and father's similar professional aspirations. My parents liked to remind me, especially at my more petulant moments, that I was named after Scarlett O'Hara from the film *Gone With the Wind* (1939), one of the first, and most impressive, technicolor films of all time. This became my favourite film, and Scarlett O'Hara, my idol. I found thrilling the idea that by playing my home movies on the VHS player plugged into our small TV with its curved glass screen and large, red plastic buttons, I could occupy the same space, walk the same ground, as Scarlett O'Hara, as well as many of my other childhood heroines. Watching Wistrand's footage, unlike Mead's, has the effect of drawing me in, allowing me to walk the same ground, implicating me in the action.

This is not my only close connection to the footage. I hardly believe this myself, but I discovered the face of my original mystery woman in Wistrand's films. In amongst the family shots of Japan where Wistrand films his wife and children there are curious interludes of him filming, rather intimately, a young, attractive woman. Apart from her having the face of my very first mystery woman, the scenes stand out because her relationship to the family is unclear and she is the only person, Western or otherwise, whom Wistrand films in close up, and the only person who speaks to Wistrand as he is filming.

There is one scene in which she appears with Wistrand's wife and children, at the Deer Park in Nara, but usually she is filmed alone, most notably in an unnamed rose garden. In this scene the head and shoulders of the mystery woman are closely tracked. Wistrand is alone with her. She wears a smart black dress and hat, looks away wistfully, then glances at the camera coyly, as if there were some secret between her and him. Several cuts later she is talking and smiling, the framing is still suggestively close, the details of her cheeks, lips, gums exposed. As she speaks to the camera silently she is flirting, goading, tempting.

I'm curious to know the identity of this woman who is identical to the first mystery woman I dreamed of, and why she is filmed so attentively, so adoringly by Wistrand. I inquired at SASE where the archivist most familiar with the collection told me that she is likely to be the sister of Wistrand's wife, Catherine, who, the archivist was told, often accompanied the family on holidays and with whom they stayed in Washington state at the outbreak of WWII. I contacted Catherine Wistrand's niece, who would be the daughter of the filmed woman, and she was very forthcoming with information about the family, telling me that her uncle had seemed a quiet, serious man and her aunt warm and funny. I emailed this niece a still shot of the woman the archivists thought could be her mother. She replied that this was definitely not so, and that she had never seen the woman in the picture before.

As I tried to rationalise it, I decided it must be that Wistrand's films are impressing themselves onto my unconscious, causing the face of my original mystery woman to be replaced with his; a trick of the psyche, a sign of my growing attachment to the footage. But the memory of this woman's face did not come to me gradually. The instant I saw her I knew she was my very first mystery woman, the prototype mystery women from which all the other versions sprang, Maya Deren included. It is not me who has appropriated Wistrand's mystery woman into my memory, but he who has taken my mystery woman into his. I can't explain how the woman I dreamed of in the 1990s has been impressed upon the face of a woman in a film from the 1930s, how my object of desire has been conflated with Wistrand's, but I know it has. My mystery woman has been taken from my unconscious and fixed in celluloid, and I don't know how to get her back.

As I reread that paragraph I realise how unhinged it could sound. I may need to take a break from the archive, focus on living people, regroup, try to forget.

Scarlett

04/09/2007

Hi Hannah,

I wonder what you're doing now and whether you've changed much in the ten years since I've been in your consulting room. My life is very much transformed since I last wrote to you - five years ago I was noticing - but I still think of you often, especially when I'm writing. In a way I think I'm still writing for you, endlessly trying to explain something.

My feelings about my mother's death have moved on now, as has my research, but I continue to read one into the other. When my mother died it was as though the larger Russian doll in which I, and my past, had been contained, was pulled away leaving me bare and vulnerable to an onslaught of memories. Something close to this experience was repeated when, six months later, my maternal grandmother died. But the attached chapter, my most recent piece of writing, is not so much about the feelings one has in the wake of a death, rather, the unexpected practical role one can find oneself in.

It has only struck me within the last few years that, unlike anyone else I have met, my mother spoke with enthusiasm about the practical consequences of her death. For as long as I can remember her future end was an open and lively topic of conversation. In my late teens and early twenties, in particular, we spent many an evening at 21 Abingdon Road, the house I had been brought up in and that she would eventually die in, drinking her acerbic and abundant home-made white wine, piffle-puffling away together while working out how I might extend or restructure the house once I had inherited it.

During these conversations, my mother would casually point out to me the storage boxes containing things that might be of interest to me: every letter written to her since 1962, the red leather knee-high boots I'd always liked but wasn't allowed to wear, the cupboards in which there was 'a load of old shit' that I should 'chuck', and where the crockery we used during my childhood had been stored, should I want it for sentimental reasons. On the mantlepiece was a document headed 'Where things are' which listed where all the important documents and items I would need after her death could be found.

All of this was in place at least two decades before she was diagnosed with lung cancer. 21 Abingdon Road had, then, for the last twenty or more years, been a living archive of the life of Joy Durand, and my mother was the highly competent live-in archivist, gatekeeper of her own life history. With all this preparation I imagined that when she died it would feel comfortable, as though she were holding my hand while I frolicked through her things, gleefully putting on the red leather boots I wasn't allowed to wear until now. Of course, when she really did die it felt nothing like that, but I like to remember the future I'd imagined.

My mother took great care to ensure that, in the event of her passing, everything would be as she wanted it. Her funeral, personal possessions, legal documents, and so on were all meticulously dealt with, wrapped up, controlled in advance by her. It is as though she expected she would be witnessing the death-related events unfold from a coma in which she would be paralyzed but cognisant (and from which she might one day awake), and couldn't bear to see things go awry, for the wrong box to be 'chucked' or an unwanted song to be played at her funeral.

The experience of my mother and grandmother's deaths, funerals, and their aftermath has taught me that when someone dies there is a kind of levelling of their life history where the most recent activities and experiences are no longer assumed to be the most relevant, as they ordinarily are during life. In a typical funeral speech, for example, the deceased's childhood and early adult life are often given more weight than the periods of their mid-life and retirement. Similarly, in the sorting of their belongings and making of an archive, the chronological time we experience in life that values 'recent-ness' gives way to an historical mode that places value on objects, documents and events according to temporally fluid criteria. Perhaps that is why, in the immediate aftermath of my mother's death, a temporal anarchy took hold in which unexpected connections and disruptions occurred, cutting across chronological hegemony and rational orders. On her death, the friends and lovers my mother had in her twenties seemed as relevant as those she had in the last ten years of her life. They were suddenly present and grieving, the letters they had sent some forty years ago seeming more alive and pertinent than her recent relationships and correspondences. My mother's birth suddenly seemed an urgent matter; a defining moment of my grandmother's life, as well as her own.

There is little preparation for these urgent matters, for

dealing with the effects of temporal anarchy and the need to make something ordered from it: One must arrange for the body to be moved and stored, record the death and obtain a certificate, find and book a venue for the funeral, write a funeral speech, respond to other mourners' questions and requests, inform the relevant bank and energy companies of the person's death, and work out what to do with their furniture, house, documents, pillows, medication and false teeth. I found myself marvelling that this labour around death is so little discussed in life, that despite my and my mother's frequent tipsy conversations about her future death, I was not at all prepared for the reality of this new role as her death-administrator, archivist, and curator of her life history.

I wonder if you would feature in my life history, if you will still seem relevant when I'm dead. I'm pretty sure I won't feature in yours. I suppose that's the nature of our relationship: you are highly significant to me and I am relatively insignificant to you, just fifty minutes of your working week, not even that anymore. Perhaps I am making our relationship more significant by writing to you like this, turning your seemingly forgotten inbox an unconsenting archive of my thoughts and struggles.

Scarlett

Handmaids

Births and deaths

Shortly following her marriage to Gregory Bateson in Singapore in 1936, Margaret Mead 'made the long sea trip to the field [Bali] to live among people who knew nothing about [her] and [her] work and regarded the whole thing—a woman going off alone to study the natives—as fantastic and reprehensible', adding that she 'had forgotten just how weird and isolating an experience it could be' (February 1936). The trip was intended to research trance or ritual possession, which Mead and Bateson hypothesised was a native manifestation of western schizophrenia (known at the time as *dementia praecox*). Much of the written material and at least half of the films in the Margaret Mead Collection record babies, small children and their mothers, reflecting the assumption that the 'schizoid type' would most likely be formed during early childhood as a result of 'pathogenic' mothering. Mead's references to babies are often made alongside references to death. 'Life swirls around us,' she writes, 'amid texts, and bad haircuts, and births of babies, and funerals' (December 1937). She writes regularly, and sometimes disturbingly, of attending cremations, which she refers to as 'a most trying kind of spectacle [. . .] one comes away with a special stench in one's nostrils, very tired, and swears that one will never go to another cremation' (December 1937). Throughout her fieldwork in Bali, Mead's camera, like her writing, appears compelled to return to the topics of babies and cremations, of birth and death.

The scene I most remember watching in the Library of Congress Motion Picture Division is of a woman apparently giving birth, lying on her back, legs stretched wide apart. Four young boys appear to be helping her. The footage is fuzzy and the camera at quite a distance but I can make out the black of her mouth occasionally opening into an agonising O. Many 'O's later a baby is flung out from between the woman's legs. It is floppy and lifeless, a gross parody of the 'limp, waxy' infants Mead saw as characteristic of the 'schizoid' type. The boys throw it around. I feel self-consciously emotional in the quiet of the Motion Picture Division viewing room. I look more closely and realise the 'baby' is a doll and the birth scene has been an enactment, a cruel trick from beyond.

> In 1946 Mother was born and her own mother, Scarlett's grandmother, entered her own particular hell. The war had treated Grandma reasonably well. Her husband was not sent away to fight, he had a good income and they lived in relative peace. Then

her husband started coming home less often, or he came home disinterested in her and smelling suspicious. She found, amidst the difficulty, that she was pregnant. But this was not all, the doctor told her. She was pregnant and she had a growth in her abdomen, possibly cancer. They could not explore until after she had given birth, but the prognosis was unlikely to be good. For six months Grandma expected a birth and a death. She waited for her D-day.

I surmise that Mead may have found this scene, like the others suggesting infant death, particularly disturbing given that she was greatly affected by the death of her nine-month-old baby sister, Catherine, in 1907, when Mead was six years old. Mead was particularly fond of this younger sister whose name she was allowed to choose. She had had a series of miscarriages in previous years, and it was in Bali, while filming these curious scenes of mothers and babies, that Mead fell pregnant with her only live child, Mary Catherine Bateson, whose middle name is the same as that of Mead's dead sister. Mary was born in New York on 8th December 1939, just after Mead had left Bali. In keeping with her scientific, or 'objective', style of anthropology, the personal significance that this apparent infant birth and death might have had for Mead goes unmentioned when the scene later enters Mead and Bateson's film *Trance and Dance in Bali*; personal anguish is repressed.

Handmaids

And here we turn to another point that Mead, and the discipline of anthropology during the early twentieth century more generally, sought to repress, namely that anthropology has been the 'handmaid of colonialism'. This phrase was so widely used during the 1960s and 70s that it is not possible to attribute it to a single author, but the sentiment behind it culminated in the development of the postcolonial theory's critique of anthropology (and psychiatry), particularly that of Edward Said, Frantz Fanon and Gayatri Spivak. It is not, however, a postcolonial critique of anthropology that I wish to pursue here, rather, a consideration of the metaphor of the 'handmaid'.

Handmaids, it seems, are a popular metaphor for critical scholars and are frequently used pejoratively, to describe unfavourable links. It has been said, for example, that the media is the handmaid of the state, the UN is the handmaid of terrorism, history is the handmaid of nationalism, and that diplomacy is the handmaid of military strategy. As valid as some of these critiques might be, one has to wonder what scholars have against handmaids. Typified as a subservient female maid of common birth who might serve as a bearer of her master's child, like Bilah to Jacob in the Old Testament, the handmaid has become a ubiquitous metaphor that implies a degree of malevolence. Perhaps what causes us to think of handmaids as disturbing figures is their embodiment of boundary-crossing, their teetering on the precarious line between private and public spheres, between inside and out, stranger and family, self and other.

Traditionally, they were employed as domestic figures, confined to the home with no rights or autonomy, and yet they were allowed to be dangerously close, perhaps physically closer than anyone, to Great Men. Children of these Great Men, indeed the Great Men themselves, may have been incubated in the wombs and fed by the breasts of these life-giving yet subservient strangers.

Margaret Atwood's novel, *The Handmaid's Tale* (1985), offers a first-person account of a handmaid's experience in the fictional totalitarian state of Gilead, which exists in an unspecified future era during which there is a return to extreme forms of patriarchy. A handmaid belongs to a 'Commander' and his infertile wife, whom she serves as a walking womb, being discarded to 'the colonies' once she is no longer able to bear children for them. In Atwood's Gilead, a handmaid does not have her own name, she is referred to as 'of' the name of the Commander to whom she belongs. The protagonist is referred to as 'Offred', as she is the handmaid of a Commander called Fred. It occurs to me that the invisibility of these handmaids, and their labour that results in a baby over which they have no claim, is similar to the invisibility of those who labour during and following a death, resulting in an archival collection over which, most often, they have no claim. In a reappropriation of the term 'handmaid', this chapter will illuminate the usually invisible labour, often undertaken by women or those with a relatively subservient role, that goes into facilitating the passage of death and the production of an archive perceived as belonging to the person who has died. We will begin with Mead and her 'Ofmeads', and then extend the discussion to other archival collections discussed in this research, and their handmaids.

Ofmeads

It is only by proxy that the deceased has a real handle on the life of their material legacy, if they can be said to at all. It is usually a partner or child of the deceased who plays the role of the handmaid, managing the movement of things from those belonging to a living person to those of an archive pertaining to a dead other. This process is doubled if a personal archive of a dead other is to be transferred to a public archive. Following her mother's instructions prior to her death, Mary Catherine Bateson donated Mead's full material legacy to the Library of Congress with open access apart from four folders that remain curiously 'restricted'. On their transfer to the Library of Congress, Mead's documents became known as 'The Margaret Mead Papers and South Pacific Ethnographic Archives', where they were ordered and gatekept mainly by Mary Wolfskill, the specialist archivist assigned to the collection, whose name garners little or no public attention. Archivists might be considered the professional counterpart of personal handmaids, toiling namelessly, in the shadows of a public archive.

> D-day did not deliver what Grandma had expected. Instead of one birth and a looming death, the 11th January 1946 hailed two births. The 'growth' was not a cancer but a

second baby, a twin. Whenever Mother told the story she would put it that she, rather than her twin brother, was thought to be cancer. Scarlett often pointed out that nobody could know which of the twins the doctor judged to be the healthy foetus and which a cancerous growth, but her mother was convinced. Cancer, it seems, punctuated the beginning and end of her life.

Even before her death, Mead was graced with a highly efficient personal handmaid in the form of her former student, Rhoda Metraux, who was her live-in partner for the last fifteen years of her life. Metraux was thirteen years Mead's junior and, it seems from the correspondence between them in the form of notes, letters and memos, was treated by Mead as though she were a hired help, a handmaid facilitating her senior years. Unlike the romantic and respectful letters to Ruth Benedict that almost always begin 'Ruth darling' and continue in a seductive tone, her notes to Metraux typically go something like 'I will return on the 20th. Please ensure that my Balinese material is to hand. I will need 5 petticoats and my frock to be collected from the dry cleaner and packed in order for me to depart on the 21st' (Box N7, folder 11 Mead Archives). The role of Metraux as a dutiful daughter, or servant, rather than an adored lover, are evident in the condolence cards she received, one of which, from the National Advisory Committee for Women, mistakenly refers to Mead as Metraux's mother, and another, from the editor of the journal *Redbook*, thanks Metraux for making Mead 'easier to work with'. Other than the unlikely presence of avant-garde filmmaker, Maya Deren, in Mead's archive, her material legacy reveals few salacious secrets. There is one letter of condolence to the executors of Mead's estate from a man who calls himself S.N. Rampal asking, among other bizarre questions, if they perhaps know whether Mead had 'any child who would have been fertilized out of my genetic fluid. . . .' Of course this is easily written off as the ramblings of a delusional fan, and should be, but it is one of the few unsavoury comments that slipped through the net. This is testament to how very meticulously gatekept Mead's archive was by Mary Catherine Bateson and Rhoda Metraux who diligently enacted Mead's posthumous wishes as though she were overseeing them from beyond the grave.

> It is nearly six months since Scarlett's mother died. Scarlett wants to dream about the woman, instead she dreams about the dead, or perhaps this amounts to the same thing. Scarlett is in her mother's house, several others are there, family mostly. It is the day of her mother's funeral but Mother is still alive. She lies propped up by pillows in her bed. She is in good spirits but ill with multiple cancers, lung the primary, as she had been in reality for the last two years of her life. Scarlett rushes around getting things ready for the service, checking the time before the hearse is due to arrive. She is concerned that her mother may not die in time

for the funeral. 'Perhaps we should postpone it,' Scarlett says. 'No sweetie,' says Mother in her deep, anodyne voice, 'you've put so much effort into planning it.' Mother assures Scarlett that she will die very soon. The hearse arrives, coffin in the back. The men in funeral attire come to collect the body and are surprised to find it still living. They carry Mother to the hearse, nonetheless. Scarlett is becoming increasingly nervous, 'I don't think you should get into the coffin, you won't be able to breathe.' Mother agrees and sits next to Scarlett on the back seat. They arrive at the crematorium more quickly than Scarlett expects. 'Maybe we should wait around the corner,' she suggests, 'you can't turn up to your own funeral alive.' Mother ignores her and steps out of the hearse. 'I'll get into the coffin and we'll keep the lid open a bit,' she says, 'nobody will notice,' she insists, 'and I'd like to hear the service.'

Ofwistrand

It was an unnamed archivist who, in 2002, drew my attention to the emergence of a new collection of footage which had made its way to the Screen Archive Southeast, one of the six regional film archives in the UK. The footage was shot by a relatively unknown Swedish diplomat,

Theodor Wistrand, who embarked on an amateur ethnography of East and Southeast Asia in the late 1930s, capturing the earliest colour footage of Korea and, we believe, of Bali, which he visited in 1939. Wistrand's films offer a curious counter-perspective to Mead's, a rainbow shadow, if you will. Mead left Bali in May 1938, so it is likely that she and Wistrand, whose travels from his home in Tokyo took him to Bali early in 1939, missed being on the island at the same time by only a matter of months. However, it appears that elements of their respective fascinations with Bali and the Balinese people with whom they came into contact, did overlap. In particular, both visitors to the island filmed the dancer I Ketut Marya, who was considered the most talented, and was certainly the most famous, individual on the Balinese dance scene. Mead notes in a letter sent from Bajoeng Gede on 28th October 1936 that she saw him dance 'and filmed him giving a first lesson - he is the most famous dancer in Bali and a gay, delightful person' (1936/1977:187), and he is even more delightful and gay in Wistrand's multicolour.

Wistrand's historically significant early colour footage of Bali and Korea had been stored in his daughter's, Sylvia Maxwell's, attic since his death in the 1950s. The 'significant' footage is on the same reels as everyday home movie footage of his wife and two daughters shot mainly during their posting in Japan during the 1930s, stay in Washington state in the 1940s, and visit to Stockholm during the 1950s. Perhaps because of this interspersing of the personal and the ethnographic, or amateur ethnographic, Wistrand's family did not imagine that the films would be of interest to a public archive, and kept them casually in their attic as family memorabilia. It was a cleaner, a handmaid of sorts, who, while she was clearing out her attic in 2002, suggested to Sylvia that rather than throwing away her late father's film canisters, she might do better to take the footage to the local film archive, the Screen Archive South East (SASE). Because of the historical significance of the early colour footage of Korea and Bali SASE, after taking in and examining the footage, offered it to the archive of the British Film Institute (BFI) who have better storage facilities. However, the BFI refused the footage because the vast majority of it was of relatively insignificant home movie scenes.

The Wistrand Collection was therefore kept and catalogued by SASE and, as part of the cataloguing and information-gathering process, Sylvia agreed to be interviewed on film by the archivists. She became a named handmaid, a bearer of information on her late father and his footage. The resulting interview footage provides the most extensive, and subjective, biographical information on Wistrand available to date. However, Sylvia's account of her father is faithfully professional, never straying from a recollection of his diplomatic career. There is no information given on his personality, his role within family life, nor his political convictions. Apart from the location of his birth, Sylvia's report of her father is the kind one might expect from a professional associate. His personal life is erased, perhaps by Sylvia's notion of propriety, or perhaps because the public figure—Wistrand the diplomat—was all his daughter came to know.

Mother fetches her box of old vinyl records from the top cupboard in which they are stored. Scarlett knows this ritual. She takes out her most prized album—*Barbara Chante Barbara* (1964). Mother says it reminds her of when she lived in Paris in 1968 and slept through the student riots. Her favourite track is Nantes which tells the tale of Barbara's father's death. Although it is never made explicit, Scarlett knows the song reminds Mother of her own father whom she knew little as he left the family to be with his secretary shortly after her and her twin brother's birth, and then died unexpectedly just before he reached retirement age. The song's story goes that Barbara and her father had been estranged for many years but he summoned her on his death bed for a final goodbye. She arrives at his house in the rain (*'Il pleut sur Nantes,'* she repeats), and carved on her memory is the room at the end of the corridor. The light was cold and white and as she entered the room, four men dressed in funeral clothing stood up. She didn't ask any questions of these strangers but she understood by their looks that it was too late. Mother places the record on the turntable, poising the needle carefully with her index finger, so that it will hit the vinyl in just the right place. There are two seconds of pre-emptive popping, like studs digging in the sand before the race starts, then the haunting vocals and precarious piano playing on track 7, *Nantes*, begin. We will now be immersed in music for four minutes and six seconds. Mother's eyes will become glassy, Scarlett will pretend she understands.

When speaking of her mother however, Sylvia often recalls personal tales which, although referencing her father, are told very much as narrations from her mother's point of view. Sylvia talks freely about her mother, mentioning that she was from a well-to-do American family who owned an island off Georgia where the latest film in the collection was shot, and that she was a fantastic hostess and socialite in the ex-patriot spheres in which they circulated. When the family moved to Tokyo, Mrs Wistrand learnt Japanese, did little housework because all the meals and cleaning were provided by servants, and became a keen still photographer, producing a large body of work that Sylvia had also kept in her attic. Sylvia becomes most animated in the interview when she tells the story of how her parents met.

> He had originally met my mother's sister in Bermuda and she had happened to mention to him that she had a sister who was going to be travelling in a couple of months to Scandinavia and she just thought it would be nice for them to meet, little did she imagine that it was

> going to be so romantic. So they met in Stockholm and after four days my father popped the question, a whirlwind romance, absolutely. But my mother, she was a bit hesitant obviously, she felt that she really didn't know my father very well although they'd seen each other non-stop for the four days she was in Stockholm. And she said well, I'll let you know, I'll write to you, you see. And then they went off to Norway and she slept on it the whole night and the next morning she decided this was it, so she wrote to say that she was accepting him, to marry him. And she always mentioned that when she went to post that letter she heard that *THUD* of the letter going down the post box and she thought, well this is my future now, this is my life.
>
> Sylvia Maxwell 2002 SASE interview

Sylvia Maxwell notes twice in her interview with SASE that she, with her mother and sister, was separated from her father for two years from 1939, while he embarked on his trip around Southeast Asia and was then stationed in Berlin immediately afterwards, not returning to his family in Washington state until 1941. It seems, though, that Wistrand was absent from his daughters even when he was present, and that in return, his daughters became an absent presence to him. Wistrand's daughters certainly take centre stage in the footage shot in domestic contexts, yet it seems that they are perhaps more comfortable being viewed through Wistrand's camera than they are interacting with him directly. Although we do not have the luxury of sound recording, there is little visible interaction between the girls and their father, and they appear to be posing by formal instruction. Sylvia speculates that the footage must have been a great comfort to her father when he was separated from the family, but does not talk about the specific contexts in which the home movie footage was shot. Like Mary Catherine Bateson's famous parents, it seems that Sylvia Maxwell's father was attempting to capture his children in a state of suspended youth, like the pre-war 'primitive' cultures he recorded as if on the brink of extinction. By looking at their daughters through a lens and recording them, might it be that for these parents, a kind of pre-emptive mourning was taking place, where their children become little lost objects to be squinted at through the frame of a viewfinder?

> Scarlett's father wants to give her a gift he has made. Two little red canvas boxes sit on the piano. When she looks closely, she can see that in the centre of each canvas, a square hole is made with a sinewy red cross stretched across it, as if to strike through what lies behind. Peering into the holes, which have been back-lit, reveals that each contains a photo of a child; one in a wood at three or four years old, the other in an industrial-looking tunnel at about eighteen months. In both images the child is alone, eerily distant, seemingly lost. She then realises that both images are photographs her father took a quarter of a century ago, they are

photographs of Scarlett. She fingers the different textures of the red boxes; the dried leaves, painted string, pebble-dashed triangles. She sees that around the edges are small gold words written in her father's hand. On the first box labelled 'Lost 1' is written 'forever lost, engrossed, uncertain, missing, presumed dead, lost, discarded, carelessly mislaid, cherished possession, thrown away'. And on the second box labelled 'Lost 2', 'dejected, irretrievable wasted, bereaved, ruined, final farewell, emptiness, love torn away, forever lost'. Her father has crossed her out, fixed her as a child-ghost, put her under erasure. He tells Scarlett, in a consolatory voice, that his art is not about her.

Towards the end of the interview with Sylvia, there is a cut to her proudly holding a framed photograph of her father sitting at a table with Mao Tse-Tung and Dag Hammarskjold, the second Secretary General to the UN, taken when Wistrand was the First Swedish Ambassador in Peking. Sylvia tells the archivists behind the camera that Wistrand negotiated the release of eleven American Airmen who had been held prisoner in China; 'He was terribly good at his job,' she says, 'he was a very good negotiator and very knowledgeable about politics and could always work something out.' Despite Sylvia's personal adulation of her father's success in this matter, I cannot find his name mentioned anywhere in public accounts of this event. An abridged version of the official story goes something like this: On 10th December 1954, the General Assembly requested the Secretary General to seek the release of eleven American airmen of the United Nations Command in Korea who were being held prisoner by The People's Republic of China. This request for the Secretary General to intercede for non-humanitarian reasons was without precedent. The situation was particularly complicated because the US had no diplomatic relations with China and were not in a good position to negotiate with them following their direction of sanctions against China during the Korean war. Being entrusted with this unprecedented and difficult task, Dag Hammarskjold adopted what he referred to as the 'Peking formula' where, because the People's Republic of China were not represented on any of the organs of the UN, it was necessary to carry out the negotiations through direct personal communication between himself and Chou En-Lai, the Foreign Minister of the People's Republic of China. Hammarskjold's novel formula proved successful when on 1st August 1955, the eleven airmen were released by the People's Republic of China. Reportedly, Chou En-Lai released the airmen in order to maintain his personal friendship with Hammarskjold and timed their release as a birthday present to the Secretary General who turned fifty on 29th July 1955. Not only does the official account erase Wistrand by leaving him completely absent, its formulation is so tied to Hammerskjold personally, that it appears impossible to write another individual, like Wistrand, into the story at all. There is little public interest in the unknown diplomat although his footage of Bali, unusual and prematurely colourful, is in some ways superior to Mead and Bateson's.

To rub the public adulation of Hammarskjold in (and Wistrand out), in 1961 the former diplomat won the Nobel Peace Prize for a series of peace-keeping acts of diplomacy, of which the release of the American airmen was the first. He did, though, win the prize posthumously, since earlier in 1961, on his way to Northern Rhodesia, Hammarskjold's plane crashed, killing him along with seven other UN staff members on board and the Swedish crew. The crash was caused by several explosions on board and it has never been established whether the crash was accidental or the plane was deliberately shot down. In contrast to Hammarskjold's dramatic end, it would seem that Wistrand rather dwindled and burnt out, during his retirement in the South of France. The archivists did not ask Sylvia how her father died, and there are no public documents available in this country reporting his death. Whatever the details, Wistrand's was a little death. It has left trails of forgotten narratives and fading images, whose illusiveness flips between the beautiful and the banal.

ZZZ

ZZZZZZZ

ZZZZZZZZZZZZ

ZZZZZZZZZZZZZZZZZZ

ZZZZZZZZZZZZ

ZZZZZZZZ

ZZZ

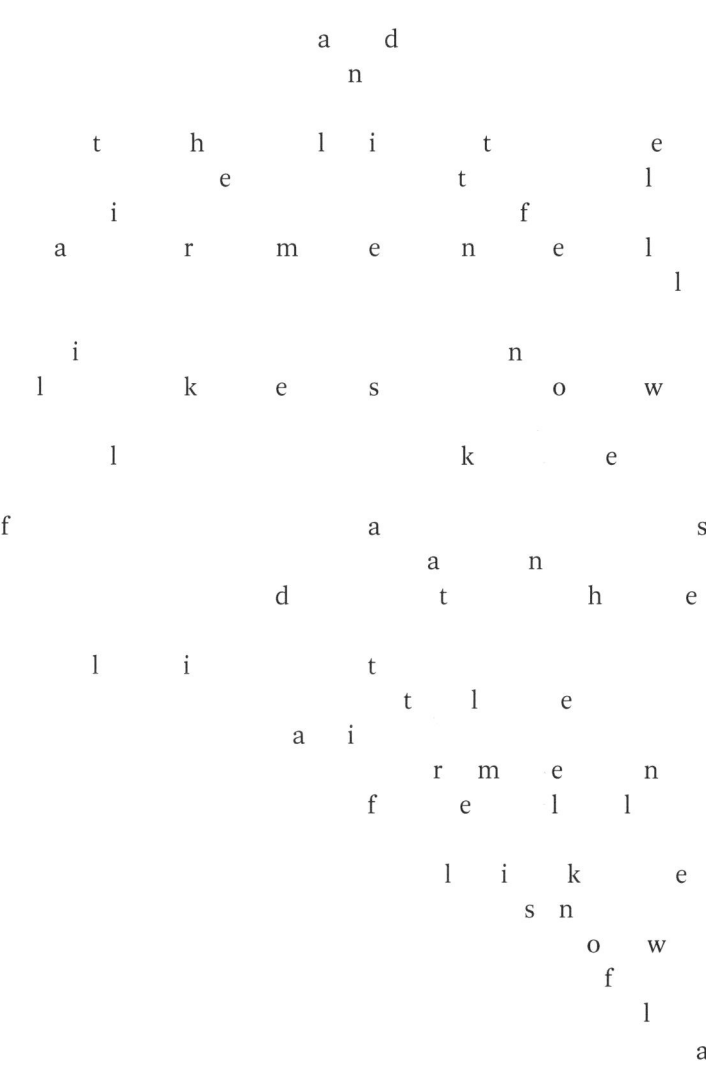

'and the little airmen fell like snowfla e s'
Scarlett's grandmother told her, sipping
her tea through creviced lips with a vintage
elegance that only those who have lived

through the early twentieth century can possess. Scarlett has heard this story before, she can recall it almost word for word: 'When I was little, maybe three or four, my mother and father saw a zeppelin in the sky near our house. It was hovering over a field. I was sleeping so they put me under the dining table to keep me safe, in case the zeppelin dropped a bomb on us. Then they woke me up and told me not to move while they went into another room to find a safe place for themselves. I couldn't help myself though, I was so curious to see what it looked like. So, I crawled out from under the dining table and looked out the window. Just as I did, I saw a brilliant light in the sky—the zeppelin was glowing in multi-colour, it was on fire. It was so beautiful. And then I noticed that all these black dots were falling from the ball of light. I didn't realise what it was at the time, but now I know; it was the little German airmen escaping from the exploding zeppelin in their parachutes. I feel so sorry for those chaps, even though they were the enemy. But it really was a beautiful spectacle as there was this ball of light in the sky and the little airmen fell like snowflakes.'

Throughout the Wistrand Collection, the man himself exists as an absent presence; present as a director, cameraman, traveller, observer but absent within the frame of view. Or almost. In the last film shot in 1952, Wistrand breaks with the fifteen-year filmic convention he has established by appearing in front of the camera. Why? After a lifetime of diplomatic service without public credit, of self-funded 'ethnographic' filmmaking that only his friends and family would watch, could this be Wistrand's last ditch attempt to be memorialized? The camera remains static, presumably he had set it up on a tripod and instructed someone to start filming at his direction. He appears in the middle of the frame, statue-like as he sits astride a large, muscular horse. Wistrand is still but sways from one side of the frame to the other as a result of the restless movements of the horse, out of shot beneath its rider. The shot lasts just a few seconds before cutting back to the regular domestic activities of the family. Following this last little monument to himself, Wistrand's biography dwindles. He leaves his films to his daughter, Sylvia, to keep in her attic, like a postcard to the future. Forty-two years later, via the hands of Sylvia's cleaner, a dusty box of celluloid secrets is delivered to SASE, an archival collection in its infancy crying out for care.

Offreud

Freud, like Wistrand, was graced with a faithful handmaid-daughter. His youngest daughter, Anna, was instrumental in the continuation of her father's psychoanalytic theories into the field of child psychology, lived with him for much of his life, nursed him in his senior years, and instructed, in her will, that their final home together at 20 Maresfield Gardens become a museum dedicated to the work of her late father. It is a lesser known fact that for forty-three years after her father's death, 20 Maresfield Gardens was the home of Anna Freud, her life-partner, Dorothy Burlingham, and Dorothy's two children to whom Anna was effectively a step-parent. During those forty-three years, Anna remained loyal to her father's view that the Oedipus complex did not predate the genital phase, as Klein and her followers asserted in opposition to Freud's theories, which resulted in the Controversial Discussions of the early 1940s, splitting the British Psychoanalytic Society into three distinct factions (the Anna Freudians, Kleinians and Independent school). Anna died in 1982 and it was in 1986, on the instructions that Anna had diligently made before her death, that 20 Maresfield Gardens was converted into the Freud Museum, as a memorial to her father.

While the Freud Museum contains, or preserves, Freud's final domestic space and consulting room, the majority of his work and related documents are held at the Library of Congress where they rub shoulders with the Margaret Mead Papers. It is perhaps a lesser-known fact that the Motion Picture Division of the Library of Congress also holds Freud's home movies, which amount to over an hour's viewing. The first video records holidays in the Alps in 1929 but the majority of the footage is shot in the 1930s when Freud appears vulnerable, pained and elderly. The final home movie is shot in the garden of 20 Maresfield Gardens on Freud's last birthday, in May 1939, after the family had been forced to transplant themselves to London following the Nazi occupation of Vienna. I viewed a copy of this footage, and was struck by the casualness of the event given the gravity of the moment in history; the end of Freud's life, and the end of many Jewish lives in Austria, and beyond.

During this sinister period, Freud was finalising for publication what is perhaps his most eccentric work, *Moses and Monotheism* (1939). This is the book that would later inspire the discussion of whether or not Freud believed psychoanalysis to be a Jewish science in Yerushalmi's *Freud's Moses* (1991) and, by extension, Derrida's *Archive Fever* (1995) to which the threat of 'radical finitude' is central; a death drive which, for Derrida, produces the feverous compulsion to record, to keep, to archive. And in *Archive Fever* there remains the wish, taken up by Yerushalmi in the concluding part of his book entitled 'Monologue with Freud', that after his death, Anna Freud would carry the spectre of her dead father. The crux of Yerushalmi's Monologue is the wish that when Anna wrote in a conference paper after Freud's death that to consider psychoanalysis a Jewish science was a badge of honour, she was speaking on her dead father's behalf, *in his name*, as she did when Freud developed jaw cancer and was unable to speak following his multiple operations.

In the Freud Museum as it is now, Sigmund Freud's consulting room remains reverently untouched, yet Anna's consulting room has been set up in another area of the house, her former bedroom and consulting room used as offices to administrate the apparently more important, paternal archive. Despite Anna's distinct contributions to psychoanalysis, particularly her founding of psychoanalytic child psychology, the name 'Freud' and house 'The Freud Museum' remains synonymous with her father. She is considered derivative; 'Anna', or 'Anna Freud' at best. She is Offreud; her father's handmaid.

Ofderrida

And here we thread back to Derrida who, like Freud, had a disciple/daughter, a handmaid carrying forward his work during his life and after his death. The handmaid I am thinking of is philosopher and critical theorist, Avital Ronell, who, by her own account in an interview she gave to *The Chronicle of Higher Education* in 2007, was a surrogate daughter to Derrida or 'his pet'. The two first met in 1979 when the young Ronell, then a performance artist in her twenties, made a memorable impression on the esteemed professor by introducing herself to him by the name of 'Metaphysics'. When, in 2004, Derrida left the doctor having been diagnosed with pancreatic cancer, which would be the cause of his death (as, incidentally, it had been Mead's in 1978), it was Ronell he immediately called. In the last few months of his life Ronell stayed with Derrida and his psychoanalyst wife, Marguerite, acting as Derrida's live-in therapist and masseuse. Despite Ronell's encouragement, he refused to hire a professional masseuse as he would not let a stranger touch him. When reflecting on the same period, Ronell recalls one instance in which Derrida awoke feeling numb and panicked. Unsure what to do, Ronell offered to brush him. Derrida agreed, although Ronell confesses that neither she nor, she suspects, Derrida, really knew what was meant by this. Making it up on the spot, Ronell found one of Marguerite's hair brushes, which she used to stroke Derrida's body until the feeling returned. In his last few weeks of life, Ronell taught Derrida to meditate despite his joking that 'my notion of meditation is Descartes'. At the end of his life, it would seem that, for Derrida, Ronell played the role of both diligent daughter and transcendental handmaid, easing the passage not of birth, but death.

> Mother had two funerals. The first was two weeks after her death and was a small service at Golders Green crematorium, attended only by family and a few close friends. The second Scarlett called a 'memorial', but in her mind it was the proper funeral, to which all Mother's friends, neighbours and exes were invited. Mother would have liked the second funeral much better than the first, which Scarlett saw as a trial run; this was fortunate as she got it wrong. When someone dies there is an immediate imperative, a kind of affront to a grieving daughter, to organize a funeral. One of the first things you have to do is find a minister, in the case of Scarlett's mother, a humanist minister, as she had clearly stipulated years before her death. This person, who you will probably have only met once before the big day and who almost certainly will have

never met the person whose funeral they are conducting, is responsible for providing the final public representation of the deceased, without rehearsal. Given the weight of the responsibility and the importance of the job they are to carry out, you would want to shop around to be sure that you choose the right person. But there is no time to do this. Once a meeting has been set up with a minister who perhaps has come recommended by someone or whose name and photo you've found on a website, there is no going back, no time to rearrange things or to change course on what you think may amount to a gross misrepresentation of the life of your loved one (as funeral ministers like to refer to dead relatives). As soon as she walked into Mandy's flat, Scarlett knew she was the wrong person for the job. Her bleached hair, pristine white carpets and pink, fluffy cushions would have deeply offended Mother's bohemian sensibilities. But there Mandy was, only nine days before the funeral, ready with her standard funeral script into which she expected Mother's life to fit.

The archive of the Ofderridas was far less organized, less controlled in advance by its maker than that with which the Ofmeads had to contend. In his last interview, for *Le Monde* in the spring of 2004, Derrida expressed his anxiety about the fate of his personal effects and writings after his death, asking 'Who is going to inherit and how? Will there even be any heirs? I leave a piece of paper behind, I go away, I die: It is impossible to escape this structure, it is the unchanging form of my life.' After they were left behind, the papers that remained in Derrida's office and attic, including books from his personal library, and later writings and letters to friends and colleagues, became the subject of a heated lawsuit. Derrida had promised the bulk of his material legacy (116 boxes and 10 oversized folders taking up 47.8 linear feet) to the library of the University of California Irvine, where he spent the last ten years of his career. However, it would seem that this donation was not enough to satisfy the University. In 2006 it came to public attention that Irvine had been in a secret dispute for two years with Derrida's widow, Marguerite, and their two sons, because of their refusal to hand over Derrida's papers and some personal effects. This was a particularly surprising move given that no formal deal had been struck between Derrida and Irvine prior to his death for the donation of either his personal papers or the ones that they already possessed. The conflict dragged to light several private secrets including, in the last few months of his life, Derrida's falling out with Irvine as a result of his writing a letter offering (allegedly unfounded) support for a colleague who had been accused of sexually harassing a student, and, in the legal paper delivered to Marguerite by a uniformed official, the existence of a third son whom Derrida had fathered with another woman. Unlike Mead, Derrida carried out little fore-planning to assist the would-be-handmaids, of his archive. 'Do they want his personal library?' asked Ronell,

'Do they want his pencils and erasures? His computer? His clothes?' What will become of Derrida's erasures? In contrast to her partner and daughter's meticulous donation of Mead's papers, photographs and films to the Library of Congress and Sylvia's donation of her father's biographical materials to a public archive, those of Ronell's dead daddy, Derridaddy, were ruthlessly prized from their domestic dwelling place. This public battle over a personal archive brought private narratives (such as Ronell's) and secrets (Derrida's and his colleague's) into the public realm of the news.

Buried within the various deaths and documents assembled in this chapter, there is the burning question of how one will be remembered, archived, or produced anew after one's death. Beyond a simple call for immortality, to be forever remembered, these various biographical narratives demonstrate a bid for the dead other to tell the story of their life posthumously, to speak as ghost. It is perhaps fitting then that the Ofderrida, the founding father of *hauntology*, will now speak of birth, death and haunting in her own name.

Ofderrida speaks, or Avital Ronell dictates

In *Dictations: On Haunted Writing* (1986), Ronell's first book, an adaptation of her PhD thesis, the life and work of perhaps the most preeminent figure of German literature, Johann Wolfgang Goethe, is traced through his haunting of subsequent thinkers, including Freud. With particular reference to his difficult birth in 1749, and his death in 1832, Ronell elucidates how he eerily spoke to and through other writers, and in so doing she hones the meaning of the term *haunted writing* which can be understood to have a manifold relationship to the figure of the handmaid. Most notably, Goethe haunted his assistant, Eckermann, who, after Goethe's death, wrote two books based on his conversations with Goethe, which are generally considered to be authored by Goethe, rather than Eckermann, despite the first being published four years after Goethe's death. In this version of haunted writing, Goethe is the Great Man, and his assistant, Eckermann, the handmaid, whose labour and name are eclipsed as though he were nothing more than a channel for the words of his master, Goethe.

Goethe's uncanny teetering on the line between presence and absence, life and death, is not exclusive to Goethe's postmortem haunting, however. In his postnatal state, Goethe was also an eerily precarious presence. After a thirty-six-hour labour, Goethe was initially believed to be still-born, as all his siblings before him had been. It was the chance presence of Goethe's maternal grandfather, Johann Wolfgang Textor, after whom Goethe was named, and who gave medical advice to the midwife, that resulted in the initially stillborn Goethe surviving. This advice was later utilized to ensure that Goethe's subsequent siblings did not die before they were born. Ronell notes that in Freud's retelling of Goethe's birth, and his written analysis of Goethe, he makes no mention of Textor, the maternal grandfather, nor the fact that Goethe was given the name of his mother's father: 'Why [Freud] had forgotten or repressed the one figure who might have furnished the gateway *(Tor)* to his own text . . . is a matter for speculation' (1986:9), writes Ronell.

> In Mandy's fluffy funeral script there were no absent fathers, pleasure from alcohol and cigarettes, running away from home at seventeen, abortions, absinthe, lesbian love affairs, studies in homeopathy that didn't amount to a career, other single mothers who acted as an adoptive family, long-standing occasional lovers, lodgers who were treated like nieces and nephews, nor unconventional hobbies like hit-and-miss DIY. Mandy asked all the wrong questions, and Scarlett was in no state to guide things. The first funeral was for a dull, fluffy woman that Scarlett did not recognise as her mother. For the memorial Scarlett found a different humanist minister who she knew Mother would have thought 'got the plot', as she used to say. During this service and wake, attended by an eclectic bunch of about a hundred of Mother's friends and associates, the mourners drank, danced and spoke freely, and the funeral service played out to the song *Nantes*.

After being taken for dead at birth, Ronell writes, '[Goethe] will want to be born again, perhaps for the first time, on his deathbed' (1986:8), for it is after his death that his life as an eminent and active ghost begins. It is clear how Goethe's ghosting, or dictating to, Eckermann allows him to be born again, but when Freud becomes involved in this spooky constellation, the dynamics of the haunting change. Freud, and by extension psychoanalysis, was undoubtedly influenced, one might say indebted, to Goethe's work yet, Ronell asserts, '[o]nly certain elements of the rapport between Freud and Goethe are admitted into the text of psychoanalysis while others necessarily remain concealed or partially unconscious' (1986:xxvii). What is of interest here is not the theoretical particulars of Goethe's influence on psychoanalysis, but Freud's mode of citing, or rather failing to cite, Goethe when the influence of his work was manifest in Freud's. Ronell describes Freud's omission, or repression, of Goethe's influence as 'a vampirization of sorts, a libidinal depletion' (1986:4). Ronell's image of vampire-Freud drinking blood, gaining sustenance, from the spectre of Goethe, resonates with the figure of the breastfeeding handmaid who namelessly feeds and gives life to an entitled baby. Within Ronell's account of Goethe's ghostly dictation, he both uses a handmaid through which to speak in his own name (in the form of his assistant Eckermann whose labour is erased in the work he produces being thought of as authored by Goethe), and becomes a handmaid of a kind in relation to Freud whose work, at times, Goethe namelessly gives sustenance to, or feeds.

Handmaids such as Rhoda Metraux, Mary Catherine Bateson, Sylvia Maxwell, Anna Freud, and Avital Ronell are crucial to the production of an archive, to the posthumous feeding of ghosts. On these typically invisible figures who act as conduits for the movement of objects and documents from the personal belongings of the living to the archival collections of the dead, the namesakes of archives are hugely dependent. The archives thought about in this chapter (Mead's, Wistrand's, Freud's, and Derrida's) can all be said to have been birthed as a result of a death. However, it is not the deceased who carries and delivers the new-born archive, rather it is a living heir who acts as a handmaid, facilitating the passage of death and namelessly giving birth to the resulting archival collection. It is on the axis of Avital Ronell's conceptualization of haunted writing that the figure of the handmaid might turn to be unshrouded, heard, and able to speak in her own name.

30-12-2009

Hi Hannah,

It has been more than ten years since I sent my first unsolicited email to you and I still haven't given up hope of a reply. I love the thrill of chancing it, taking a gamble on whether or not you will one day open our old inbox, read my messages and write back. Sometimes I check my spam folder, just in case a reply from you has accidentally slipped into it. I've come to think that technological 'accidents' are rarely that; they have power and meaning, like a Freudian slip in speech, like my mystery woman slipping into the Wistrand Collection.

These days I see all technology as haunted: phones, emails, film, photography, all conduits that can have the effect of bringing the dead to life, or rendering the living ghostly. Fran and I got back together nine years ago and in my wallet I still have the passport photo of her I took with me to DC in 1997, more than twelve years ago now. When I look at the photo, I don't see the living Fran I am in a relationship with currently, I see the Fran I left in 1997, who is now dead. Dead Fran lives in my wallet, living Fran in my house. The inverse happens when I look back over my old emails to you from DC and read what I wrote to you about my mother. It is as though she is living again, not that she is brought back from the dead, but that I am brought back to her, returned to her living past.

I think I had begun to memorialize my mother in writing, to produce her as a ghost, before she was diagnosed with the lung cancer that resulted in her death. Part of me knew what was coming, that she couldn't get away with her 'little piffle-puffles', as she affectionately called her chain of thin, hand-rolled cigarettes, for much longer. She also knew so herself, often saying irreverently and without regret that she had chosen the proverbial 'short and happy life' over the long and miserable one she imagined denying herself cigarettes would bring.

Sometimes I think she had a point and I consider starting to smoke again. I contemplate committing a slow suicide, gradually administering a poison that means I'm likely to die before I become incontinent, incapacitated or senile. Fran does not agree with this sentiment, she says she needs me alive, even if I am incontinent, incapacitated and senile.

I wonder if you have someone strong and sensible, like Fran, in your life. I like to think that you do.

I may not write again for some time.
Scarlett

Part III:
Posthumous Emails
2021 & 2011

. . . the phantom continues to speak . . . a bit like the answer machine whose voice outlives its moment of recording: you call, the other person is dead, now, whether you know it or not, and the voice responds to you, in a very precise fashion, sometimes cheerfully, it instructs you. . . .

Jacques Derrida, *Archive Fever* (1995)

10/01/2021

Dear Scarlett,

I hope this email finds you well, despite the difficulties and restraints we are all currently facing.

I must apologise for only replying to your emails now, eleven years after the last one was sent. I had not looked at the account I set up for you while you were away in DC since you ended the therapy in 1997, as it was my understanding that you would contact me by phone on my usual number should you wish to make contact. It was only a week ago, when I received an automated email about the account needing to be recovered, that I found the emails you sent in subsequent years.

I read your emails last week and I found them very moving. I expect you may have felt rejected after writing to me repeatedly with such care and openness, without receiving a reply. I hope this email, though tardy, goes some way to repairing any pain my lack of response may have caused you.

I also wanted to say that, although it is a relatively long time ago now, I am so sorry to learn of your mother's death. She had become - you had made her - very vivid in my mind.

With best wishes,
Hannah

12/01/2021

Hi Hannah,

This is Fran. We haven't met but I think you know who I am. I was Scarlett's partner and she spoke about me in therapy. I'm managing her email account now.

I have some bad news about Scarlett. Sorry if this sounds blunt, but she died in 2011. To be honest, Scarlett's death and the fallout from it has taken up the last ten years of my life and I'm tired of dealing with it. You may not know that we got back together in 2000 and had twins in 2002. Because Scarlett died intestate, I had a five-year legal battle to try to keep our family home and savings which came from the proceeds of Scarlett's mother's house and were all in Scarlett's name. Had we been a straight couple, her estate would have automatically passed to me and the kids but because we couldn't get married - same-sex marriage was not legally recognised until 2014 - I had no legal right to her estate. Neither did the children because I carried them - Scarlett used to joke that I was her 'handmaid'! Jokes aside, that meant that Scarlett wasn't the twins' legal parent as two same-sex parents weren't allowed on the birth certificate at that point, and because they weren't her legal children, they had no legal claim to her estate. All that philosophising about death, archives and estates left in a mess, and she didn't sort out her own will. As it turned out this was no laughing matter as we've ended up with half of what we took for granted as our family's property and money when

Scarlett was alive, and the rest has gone to 'blood' relatives whom she barely knew and certainly wouldn't have wanted to leave anything to.

Anyway, I'm taking the time to write back to you because I know you meant a lot to Scarlett, and maybe she meant a lot to you too. I know it's probably unethical or whatever, but after Scarlett died, I logged into her email account and read most of her messages, including the 'therapy' emails between you while Scarlett was in DC and we had split up for a while. When I first read them I was really pissed off at the whole 'illicit' thing between you. It seemed like you were more exciting to her than I was at that time, like you were the one who could really understand her and her crazy 'mystery woman' dreams. Although Scarlett said she was sure you were straight it felt like you were the other woman. But then after a while my view mellowed. I can see from the emails that you were very caring and patient with Scarlett, more patient than I was, but then you probably never saw how she could be at her worst. It's a shame you didn't write back to Scarlett before she died. She always hoped you would.

I can see Scarlett sent you two of her chapters. I don't know why she didn't send you the last one she wrote, in that year before she died. Maybe it shows a side of her she didn't want you to see - her more fucked up, rebellious side. I've only skimmed it myself - it always creeps me out reading her work - but if you want to read it, I'll send it to you. I could tell you a lot about Scarlett and her life that I think you'd be interested to hear. I'd be interested to know what she said about me and our relationship during her in-person therapy before she went to DC. I was thinking maybe we could exchange what we know about her over the phone or zoom? I'm always giving out information about Scarlett to other people, it would feel good to actually be given some new information about her from someone else for a change.

Let me know.
Fran

25/01/21

Dear Fran,

Thank you for taking the time to write to me and for letting me know of Scarlett's death. That is very sad and shocking news. I'm so sorry for your loss, and for the difficulties you and your children have faced following it. My sincerest condolences.

Thank you for your offer of sending me the last chapter Scarlett wrote and meeting over phone/zoom to talk about her. I have given the ethics of this is very unusual situation a lot of careful thought. I understand that it may give you comfort to hear new information from me about Scarlett, however I'm sorry that I will not be able to do that. It would be a breach of my professional code of conduct, and of Scarlett's confidentiality, for me to share with you what we talked about during her psychotherapy sessions. I hope you understand.

As you are not bound by any professional codes of conduct, it is up to you what you share of Scarlett's life with me, and if you would like to send me the chapter you mention then I would be happy to read it.

If it's not too painful for you to repeat it, could I ask how she died?

Please accept, once again, my belated condolences.

Best wishes,
Hannah

26/01/2021

Hi Hannah,

I thought you would say that. It's a shitty role I'm in where I have to endlessly give out information about Scarlett's life to other people and get nothing from them in return. Well, here we go again.

She died in a car crash on 25th September 2011. It was a weird time as she'd been increasingly obsessed by coincidences, or what she called 'synchronicity', in the three years leading up to the crash. I wanted her to see a therapist about it - I asked her to call you actually - but she refused. Said she liked the gamble of only writing to you at your old email address and seeing what would happen. I thought she was losing it but Scarlett thought things were finally making sense. I'm still not sure which of us was right.

It started with this new colour footage she found in 2002 - the Wistrand Collection. At first it was just about comparing the colour footage from Bali with Mead's black and white footage as they were shot around the same time, which made sense. But then she said she found 'her' mystery woman in his films and she started to see the footage as 'haunted'. That's when things started to go awry. She became obsessed by some earlier footage Wistrand shot in Japan and convinced herself that the film was speaking to her by turning red - she called it 'bleeding' - and that it somehow all connected to that haemorrhaging trauma from her teens, which she talked to you about in therapy, I think. I'm a meteorologist, my background is in the physical sciences, so the whole idea of the unconscious and connections between things that can't be proven or even seen is lost on me. Scarlett and I didn't really connect over her work, we had other things in common. But you probably already know that. Scarlett always used to say it was strange that you knew so much about her and she knew so little about you. Now I'm starting to understand how she felt.

Anyway, you asked how she died. She was driving up the M40 on her way to a writing retreat in Oxfordshire where she was going to write the remaining two chapters she had planned and finally turn her research in DC, and later at SASE, into a book. At the time of the crash it was dark and there was convectional rainfall, so visibility would have been poor. That probably contributed to her accident. Eye witnesses say she was changing into the fast lane when her car spun out of control, smashing into the metal crash barrier. It was recorded as a death by road accident with 'external road environment' and 'driving too fast for the conditions' as contributory factors. I objected to last factor because it made it sound like the accident was Scarlett's fault and I didn't want the twins thinking that. But the coroner insisted it stayed there as, according to speed cameras, she was driving at 73mph which is considered 'too fast' when it's dark and raining. It made me really angry at the time, but I've come to accept the death record now.

So, Scarlett's final 'red' chapter is attached. I'd be interested to know, as a psychotherapist, what you think of it, if you're allowed to tell me, that is... By the way, I remember Scarlett saying that you'd either love or hate it. She said she wondered whether you'd think she was finally speaking in her own name or just making a show of speaking in other people's. You'll probably understand better than I do what that means.

All best,
Fran

Seeing Red, Hearing the Dead

My Mother.

I'm in love with red. I dream in red.

My nightmares are based on red. Red's the color of passion, of joy. Red's the color of all the journeys which are interior, the color of hidden flesh, of the depths and recesses of the unconscious. Above all, red is the color of rage and violence.

Kathy Acker, *My Mother: Of Demonology* (1993)

When Avital Ronell was invited by Amy Scholder to contribute to a posthumous volume on her friend, the punk writer Kathy Acker, she was split: 'I was very pleased but I was split. I am tempted to say right now, at this early stage of my reflections on Acker, "end of story: I was split", story of my life, Amy invited me, I was split—I was simply inclined to bail, to leave' (2006:16). The ensuing essay does not attempt to eulogize nor memorialize, rather, Ronell's 'Kathy Goes To Hell: On the Irresolvable Stupidity of Acker's Death', a play on Acker's 1978 novel *Kathy Goes to Haiti*, unfolds as a piece of haunted writing. Ronell claims that if she were Kathy the resulting text would, instead, have emerged as a kind of 'spliterature', splitting up with no origin and no end (2006:16). In a sense, she is and it does. For Ronell, splits appear in a number of different guises, and proliferate both within and between her and Kathy. These splits, like their *differend* on the issue of Martin Heidegger, for example, are immutably connected with their long-standing close friendship and the loss Ronell feels as a result of Acker's death in 2001. But I want to take this short piece of spliterature as an axis upon which to explore other kinds of splits; the splits are shared by and played out through the various channels (and the ghosts they relay and relate with) in this chapter.

Historiographically speaking, any act of textual production concerning the past could be understood as a form of channelling, of conjuring the dead and bringing them into an artificial state of being. In this chapter I am turning on and tuning in to the very first films Wistrand made (shot during his trips around Japan and China in 1937-8), and considering myself a kind of channel. Of course channels, like mediums, are never neutral. They select, edit and interfere with their transmissions. In so doing, channels are active agents which might be understood as being in a relationship with whatever (or whoever) they transmit. An objective here is to consider the nature of my relationship to (or perhaps *with*) Wistrand, which might be comparable to Ronell's with Acker in the aforementioned haunted writing.

I want to approach myself and Ronell as channels, Acker and Wistrand as the ghosts we transmit, and 'Kathy Goes to Hell' and this book as the end-products of the transmissions. In the terms of this line of thought, the third channel we are to investigate is historian Iris Chang, transmitting the victims of the Nanking Massacre of 1937, in her book *The Rape of Nanking* (1997). Of course, these three channels have not been arbitrarily chosen, nor do they operate in parallel to each other, although there are parallels to be drawn. Rather, they have been selected for their thematic and biographical (dis)connectedness, so that in what will follow, they run in conversation and at interference with each other. They have been deliberately spliced together to split up the presumed line of enquiry, the medium from the ghost, the channel from the transmission.

> Like many early teenage years, Scarlett's were bound to a highly narcissistic friendship. She and Sadie were one and the same from the ages of 11 to 15. They were best friends. At their age, that was code for narcissistically intertwined. Their parents had to accept that if they had their daughter at home, they also had her double. For Scarlett, spending time with Sadie was like spending time with her own reflection. They even sounded and looked nearly identical. At school people used to mix them up, like twins. The split occurred when, at 15, they were each seduced by different worlds.

Coming from an aristocratic family, Sadie rebelled by sleeping around with the 'baddest' boys in West London—a smorgasbord of truants, pot heads, coke heads, pill heads, drug dealers, Triads, arms dealers and pirate radio DJs with a penchant for domestic violence. Some of these characters they had befriended jointly, but Scarlett quickly tired of them and turned to an eclectic bunch of older artists for stimulation. In the summer after they finished school and before they would go to different sixth-form colleges, Scarlett went on holiday with Sadie, her new best friend, Lisa, and three of their least 'bad' 16-year-old boyfriends. The choice of location was not Scarlett's: they were to stay on the Isle of Cumbrae, off the west coast of Scotland, not in the grand 17-bedroom mansion Sadie's family owned, but in the local caravan park, to prove to the local boys that they weren't snobs. Coming from far humbler stock than Sadie, Scarlett did not feel an imperative to prove this point. Things went smoothly, predictably at least, until the wee hours of their second night. With Sadie and Lisa off shagging whatever-their-names-were in the boys' caravan, Scarlett was left in the girls' caravan with the remaining boy, to whom she came to realise she had been sexually betrothed.

As they had not put any money in the pay-as-you-go meter, there was no electricity. More bored than aroused, Scarlett took advantage of the darkness to fantasise whatever she desired, while he took advantage of her body. Once they got to the stage of fumbling in the dark for a condom, Scarlett could no longer maintain her imagined scenario. She stopped, got up off the bed they were in, and made her way into the next-door bedroom. The boy followed her for an explanation, understandably. The words that Scarlett found coming from her mouth were; 'This is ridiculous, we can't have sex, I mean, *I'm more like your mother than your lover.*' Curiously, given that they were the same age, the boy accepted this without dispute and kindly agreed to go and put some money in the electricity meter so that they wouldn't have to sit in the dark anymore. What he came back to, I suspect, continues to haunt him.

I play Wistrand's films again, in silence as the first inter-title appears; 'A Stroll Through the Parks and Streets of Tokyo'. The very first image that appears through Wistrand's lens is a long-shot of a mother walking along the side of the street, whilst carrying her baby in a sling around her side. Wistrand quickly pans left to reveal an urban road with oncoming cyclists and pedestrians. As if this were an unintended beginning, after only two seconds the scene is cut and we return to the point from which the previous shot started with a similar but different mother and child walking towards the camera from a slightly further distance than the pair before. Wistrand's wife, Catherine, then appears from the right of the screen, walking into shot down the road with her back to the camera. Again Wistrand pans left, away from his wife's body and leaving the Japanese mother and child out of shot. Once at quite a distance from her husband, and nearly also out of shot at the far right of the screen, Catherine looks back at the camera. At this point Wistrand promptly cuts the scene to a closer image of his wife's back, as if to avoid overt acknowledgement of his presence. But I don't want the scene to be cut there. I want to see more of his wife's interaction with him, and to go back to the mother and child, to see them in close-up.

A series of street and park scenes follow, in which the camera moves hesitantly from right to left and back again, capturing the crowds, but never lingering for long enough on the individual faces that emerge from them. Wistrand repeatedly pans upwards, away from faces and towards the tops of trees, cherry trees I later discovered. What Wistrand was filming was a Hanami—a Japanese festival in celebration of flowers, specifically cherry blossoms at that time of year, most likely April-May. The cherry blossom and crowds of Japanese celebrants are interspersed with shots of a temple, river, and occasionally Catherine, who most often looks upwards at the blossoms, which prompts the camera to follow. The first of Wistrand's films are typical tourist images of a Japanese Hanami. They are light amateur entertainment suited to family viewing, afternoon tea and polite conversation. This is not the story I want. I feel compelled to take Wistrand's camera and point it somewhere else, to violently snatch it from him and bring all this frivolity to a bloody end.

The majority of the films Wistrand made are shot on colour Kodachrome reversal film. Owing to the high-quality tonal range and longevity of this medium, much of the footage from the collection has retained its colour definition to a standard near that of the time it was shot. For this reason, an archivist from SASE described Kodachrome to me as 'absolutely magic film'. Wistrand's films no doubt possess a magical quality, but perhaps for additional, even oppositional, reasons to those the archivist suggested. Kodak first introduced Kodachrome film to the market in 1935 which remained the superior choice in colour film for both amateurs and professionals for decades after. However, it was not until improvements made by Kodak in 1938 that Kodachrome film achieved the level of notable stability it is most commonly thought to possess. Unlike its descendants, the stock produced between 1935 and 1938 is very prone to fading. Consequently, the earliest footage Wistrand shot (1937-8), while he was stationed in Tokyo as the First Secretary to the Japanese Swedish Legation, has significantly deteriorated in verisimilar colour accuracy. What I want to suggest is that by paying attention to the film stock and its decay, rather than purely to the images it was used to record, repressed histories might emerge.

While the Wistrands were in Tokyo enjoying the extravagances of a diplomatic lifestyle, the Japanese were invading China, leading to a full-scale war between the two countries by the summer of 1937. In December 1937, the violence escalated into what is arguably one of the most brutal episodes of recorded history—the Nanking Massacre. Also known as the 'forgotten holocaust', the numbers of those killed at Nanking are estimated at 300,000—more than the death tolls of Hiroshima and Nagasaki combined, yet prior to Iris Chang's landmark book on the massacre in 1997, there was little public or academic engagement with the event.

Like myself and Ronell, Chang is not a neutral channel for the dissemination of information on Nanking. Her research and the resulting book, which is concerned not merely with recounting historical events but with considering the processes through which histories are written, or written out ('How does an event like the Rape of Nanking vanish from Japan's (and even the world's) collective memory?', she exclaims), is driven by personal investment and plagued with the trappings this produces. As a child, Chang's parents and grandparents, who had grown up in China during World War II and escaped the city of Nanking just before the Japanese invaded, told her stories of the Sino-Japanese War so that they would not be forgotten. In particular, they did not want her to forget the Rape of Nanking. Chang recollects that with 'their voices quivering with outrage', her parents told her of the atrocities at Nanking and how the Yangtze River, which semi-encircles the city, 'ran red with blood for days' (1997:8). Chang explains that throughout her childhood, the Nanking Massacre 'remained buried in the back of [her] mind as a metaphor for unspeakable evil' (1997:8), but that her concern with the events of 1937 faded as she entered adulthood. It was not until she attended a conference in 1994, in which the victims of Nanking were commemorated using visual material including 'some of the most gruesome photographs I had ever seen in my life' (1997:9), that Chang's interest was rekindled. This prompted her to begin researching the massacre in an academic capacity, leading to the publication in 1997, of *The Rape of Nanking: The forgotten holocaust of World War II* which, in the English-speaking world, remains the authority, and best-selling book, on the Nanking Massacre.

From the Japanese and Chinese flags and presence of the red cross, to the bloodied streets and river, the scarlet lanterns used to light the dark interiors of the city whose exterior burned in the night, the imagery surrounding the Nanking Massacre in accounts like Chang's, is overwhelmingly drenched in red. A Japanese photojournalist Kawano Hiroki who was present in Nanking at the start of the massacre commented; 'I remember there was a pond just outside Nanking. It looked like a sea of blood—with splendid colours. If only I had colour film . . . what a shocking shot that would have been!' Like this photojournalist, Chang saw red, and red, it seems, is the colour of the Nanking Massacre.

With recourse to the decay of Wistrand's films shot in geographically proximate areas during the massacre, I also see red. His use of Kodak's unstable early Kodachrome film to record his extensive travels, in urban and rural Japan from 1937-8, has resulted in these first nine of his eighteen films having adopted an uncanny aesthetic. Kodachrome film is composed of cyan, yellow and magenta gelatine layers which each decay at different rates, depending on which is more exposed. This is what causes the film to appear tinted. As a result of this form of decay, the cyan and yellow layers of Wistrand's Japanese footage have faded, leaving the Japanese films marked by a distinctly crimson hue, as though, through time, the blood of the Chinese victims has seeped to the fore. In my transmission of the departed Wistrand, the redness of his early films represents the latent reality of the massacre that he failed to consciously document in his recordings. If its organic developments are understood as film's unconscious processes that might undercut the conscious intentions of the film maker, then it is in the form of the colour red that the Nanking Massacre is abstractly bleeding its way out of repression (invisibility), into the films' conscious (visible) life. It is in the colour red that a split from Wistrand's original transmission might be enacted. Red also taints Ronell's transmission. In the last lines of 'Kathy Goes to Hell', subheaded '8. Ugh!', Ronell notes that '[Acker's] unconscious turns up in red'. In doing so she comes, albeit briefly, to a new posthumous understanding of her friend based on Kathy's 'romanced red', which undercuts the authority of the preceding essay. We are left, as with the decay of Wistrand's films and the bitterness of Chang's parents' memories, with a pervading sense of something unfinished. The hauntings continue, ghosts speaking through and disturbing their channels, particularly through the uncanny redolence of the colour red.

'Kathy Goes to Hell' unfolds not only as reflection on Ronell and Acker's friendship, but as a meditation on the philosophy of friendship and loss. In recalling her friend, Ronell begins with citation. Without using the language of channelling I have adopted here, but preminiscent of it, Ronell sees citation, her fragile point of entry, as a way of calling to the other, as 'an address to Kathy, from Kathy, to you, through me' (2006:14). Although Acker remained a 'loyal daughter' to the philosophical lineage to which she often referred, Acker pissed on the boundary between citation and plagiarism. For Ronell, a large part of the effective radicalism of Acker's writing rested in her undermining of 'the staple myths of originality, of literary ownership and reliable reference' (2006:23), as she pilfered, violently snatched and snapped up titles and prose from the works of others, to claim them momentarily as her own. Ronell points out that citation is always linked to memory and, with recourse to Derrida, that it offers the possibility of a *post mortem* discourse (2006:14). It is apt, then, that by citing and reciting Acker in 'Kathy Goes to Hell', Ronell's voice at times becomes implicitly enmeshed with her dead friend's. More explicitly, Ronell relates how, in her day to day life, she has partially incorporated Kathy's voice. A true neurotic, Ronell has installed sound systems through which Kathy booms words, and it has sometimes been surprising to receive her dictations.

> I am talking to the dean on behalf of my department and the word "cunt" comes up mid-sentence, in Kathy tonalities ("we're requesting additional funding for a visiting CUNT professor")....
> Ronell 2006:24

A section of Acker's *My Mother: Demonology, A Novel* is dedicated '(to B who is dead.)'. For Ronell, 'B' is a cipher for Being and throughout the book Kathy is 'writing to the dead, dedicating to the dead, making friends, conversing with the departed' (2006:32). But, of course, through this citation, Ronell could also be writing about her own endeavour in the project she is undertaking. Wistrand and I lack the linguistic relationship held between Acker and Ronell, but share the bond of citation. This project of written re-assemblage, of re-citing Wistrand's material legacy, has demanded that I enter into a post mortem discourse with him. By setting him up to disrupt, converse and compete with the voices of others, I have become the channel through which Wistrand might posthumously speak in a performance of morbid ventriloquism. What remains unclear in this act, as with all the various channels' summonsing of the voices of the dead, is who is ventriloquising whom.

My desire not to see Japan and China in 1937 only as Wistrand recorded it, has left me an open channel to other ghosts. Chang is something of a double agent. Undoubtedly she is a channel for the victims of the Nanking Massacre but also, following her death in 2004, she has herself become a ghost. When I first came to research the Nanking Massacre, however, I mistook her as neither channel nor ghost, treating her merely as the author of my primary (although secondary) source (*The Rape of Nanking* 1997). She duly ventriloquised me. Unable to split my voice from hers, everything I wrote about the massacre came out in Chang's didactic tone. I became unable to see the events of 1937 in any way other than through her red-tinted glasses. And I still haven't been able to shake those glasses off. But at least now I know they're there. So, teetering on that precarious line between citation and plagiarism, paraphrasing and copying, this is Chang, speaking through me, on the Rape of Nanking:

> In November 1937 three parallel squads of Japanese troops marched on the city of Nanking. By approaching from a southeasterly direction in a semi-circular formation, the army took advantage of Nanking's position in the crook of a northward to eastward bend in the Yangtze river, using the water as a natural barrier to entrap the inhabitants of the city. In the early predawn hours of December 13th, fifty thousand Japanese soldiers smashed through Nanking's walls. Surprisingly, the Japanese army were vastly outnumbered by the Chinese trapped in Nanking who, historians have estimated, amounted to more than half a million civilians and ninety thousand troops. In order to defeat the numerous Chinese, the Japanese employed methods of deception, most notably by offering the Chinese fair treatment in exchange for non-resistance. Contrary to the expectations of the Japanese (who knew that the Chinese would be capable of overthrowing their army if they chose to revolt), the Chinese fully complied. Resistance was almost non-existent and the Chinese troops handed themselves over as prisoners of war.

> Becuse the Samurai culture of the Japanese military upheld dying for your leader as the ultimate honour, and saw suicide as preferable to surrender, the

non-resistant actions of the Chinese enraged and disgusted the Japanese troops. As a result, they regarded the Chinese as non-human, and came to refer to them as pigs. Azuma Shiro, a Japanese soldier, wrote in his diary 'a pig is more valuable now than the life of a [Chinese] human being. That is because a pig is edible'. Because of the ideology developed in Nanking that the Chinese people were less valuable than animals, the usual rules of military conduct with respect to the enemy were disregarded by the Japanese. Groups of Chinese soldiers were promised humane treatment so complied with the Japanese army who rounded them up into groups of several hundred, supposedly to be taken to POW camps. These groups were not taken anywhere but were gunned down on the spot, tortured, or used for bayonet practice. The violence and killings were concentrated in the first 6-8 weeks of Japan's occupation of Nanking. During this time, it has been reported by former Japanese soldiers, that the atrocities committed included putting Chinese civilians into killing lines where those in the second row were forced to behead those in the first row, and throw the decapitated bodies in the river before they were beheaded by the third row, and impaling babies on bayonets then tossing them, still alive, into pots of boiling water. It has been estimated that at least 260,000 non-combatants died at Nanking, mainly in these few weeks from late 1937 to early 1938, some estimate over 350,000.

The Nanking Massacre has also been dubbed 'The Rape of Nanking' because the violence took a particularly sexual nature, with at least 20,000 women being raped during its course. Many of these women were gang raped until they died from vaginal haemorrhaging, some were raped by their own fathers, brothers or sons who were forced to carry out sexual acts on their female relatives at the gun or knife point of Japanese soldiers. As a consequence of the Japanese soldiers' rape of large numbers of local women, the Japanese high command set up an underground network of 'Comfort Houses' in which the soldiers could 'relieve themselves' without officially breaching the rules of military conduct. The first Comfort House near Nanking was opened in 1938. Like the others of its kind, it was a sordid brothel with extremely poor sanitation in which resided the 'Comfort Women' who the Japanese soldiers came to refer to as 'public toilets'. These women were most often forcibly recruited into prostitution from either local areas or, more commonly, from the Japanese colony of Korea, and also from China, Taiwan, the Philippines and Indonesia. Mortality rates among the comfort women were high as a result of disease from poor sanitation, murder perpetrated by the Japanese soldiers, or suicide, particularly by those women who came from Asian Confucianist traditions where a great deal of importance was placed on chastity.

Despite the large numbers killed, and the particularly violent ways in which many of the Chinese victims met their end, the Nanking Massacre has been little researched or publicly discussed. Unlike the German government in relation to the Holocaust, no official apology has been made by the Japanese to the Chinese for the Nanking Massacre, nor any reparations given to the victims or their families. Although in 1937 the atrocities being committed in Nanking were well reported to a world audience, public interest in the occurrences there quickly dwindled and many of its perpetrators remained in office for decades after without punishment, reprimand or trial. To this day, Japanese academics shy away from researching or publishing on the Rape of Nanking, and many of those who deny the Rape of Nanking altogether are still in Professorial positions in prominent Japanese universities, most notably, Professor Nobukatsu Fujioka of Tokyo University. In 1997, Fujioka published two volumes, *History the Textbooks do not Teach* and *Shameful Modern History*, in which he 'corrected' what he referred to as Japan's 'dark history'. Both volumes were in the top ten books sold in Japan that year. In 2000, Fujioka and others formed the Japanese Society for History Textbook Reform, which seeks to remove war time atrocities perpetrated by Japan (such as the Rape of Nanking) from history text books in an effort to increase the population's national pride. According to Fujioka, the comfort women were voluntary prostitutes, and he referred to the money they received from Japanese soldiers as 'hitting the lottery'. Fujioka, like many Japanese neonationalist scholars, attempts to debunk the many testimonies of comfort women that appeared in the 1990s on the grounds that their claims cannot be positively verified (despite scores of similar accounts from various former comfort women).

Kathy was aware of the levels of stupor that
universities are capable of dispensing; sometimes she needed it and found the stupifying
nature of teaching to bring comfort. As far as
Kathy was concerned – and she was not alone
in this – universities have peculiar transmission problems: they transmit stupidity.
Ronell 2006:15

Interestingly, Fujioka is willing to drop his positivist stance in the service of building national pride. When writing Japanese history textbooks that do not contain 'dark secrets' like the Nanking Massacre, Fujioka adopts a postmodern rhetoric to justify his methods stating that 'To write [a history] based only on verified historical truths makes . . . [it] insipid and dry. I changed my policy for the lack of an alternative—I had no choice but to write from my own imagination to a great extent'. The typically postmodernist use of 'history as story' seems at odds with the modernist project of nation building. However, the two seem to sit together very effectively for the best-selling Fujioka. As Nozaki (2005) points out, this 'is a clever move for neonationalists, and one that is worrisome for progressive/feminist historians. For, if neonationalists are unable to win the battle over empirical research and testimony, perhaps they can win with fictional narratives appealing to the national pride and patriotic spirit'. This also poses problems for the direction in which we have embarked, for a journey into the realms of the (filmic) unconscious, driven by posthumous imaginings, must be at least semi-fictive and therefore falsifiable. Could the kind of fictive truth discussed in *Archive Fever* in relation to Yerushalmi's 'Monologue with Freud' and produced here through Acker-esque plagiarism and Ronell-esque chanelling, amount to something malign? As voices of the dead compete, it becomes hard to separate one from the other, to split them apart. A ghost's story might become tainted with that of another. Here again, Chang haunts my transmission of Wistrand:

> It is hard to guess, impossible to know and easy to imagine, what Wistrand's awareness was of the massacre that was being perpetrated by the army under whose government he was protected. Wistrand did visit China under Japanese protection in 1937/8, filming in the Forbidden City, but not in Nanking as far as we can tell. Nonetheless, he may well have visited there. In February 1938 many foreign diplomats were invited to the Japanese embassy in Nanking where glamorous receptions and media events were held to detract attention from the recent massacre. At a tea to which a group of foreign diplomats were

invited, a Japanese general boasted that the Japanese army was highly disciplined, and that not a single violation of this discipline had occurred during the Russo-Japanese War and Manchurian campaign, adding that if any atrocities had occurred in Nanking, it was because under the order of the International Safety Zone Committee (which we will return to later), the Chinese had resisted (Chang 1997:152). The Japanese media circus in Nanking certainly did not fool all of the foreign diplomats. One German diplomat, for example, noticed that while the gala was taking place 'a mother of an 11-year-old girl who did not want to release the young girl to be raped by the Japanese soldiers was burnt down with her house'. If Wistrand was one of the foreign diplomats invited to Nanking it might be surmised that he, particularly being stationed within Japan, was also privy to some of the atrocities taking place and, like the rest of the international diplomatic community, did nothing to stop them.

> Under the bright neon lights which all came on at once, as if to glare at some irrepressible truth, were paths of red across the white floors and bed linen. Lines of blood that had seeped from her cunt. Trailing from the living area where the fornication began, to the main bedroom where they had fumbled for contraception in the dark, through the caravan's hall, into the second bedroom where

> Scarlett had explained her refusal, were crimson excretions. Bold and brazen as murder. And there she still sat, on a starched white sheet, silent with shock, in a pool of red.

When I first met Acker, it was as if memory, mother of Muses, had been engaged in advance. I had already read her, begun the process of introjection according to a private transferential bureaucracy of self, and remembered her. There was something ass-backwards about our encounter, which occurred as a kind of material extension of a friendship already begun—a constellated relationship already capable of its idiomatic quarrels and turns, complicates and rushes. As in any number of transferential engagements, Kathy proceeded herself in my life and already occupied an internal territory of considerable consequence.
(Ronell 2006:14)

Avital and Kathy 'hung out' together (1996:16), they were friends, they spent time in each other's company, they hung out. But the friendship has a before and an after to the time and space they jointly encountered. Ronell's writing makes evident that after Kathy's death, since they split, they continue to speak through and to each other, and that before they met, their friendship had already begun, manifest through Ronell's process of introjection on reading Acker's work. This means that a friendship can begin through a one-way textual engagement in accordance with one's private transferential bureaucracy of self, and can continue in that fashion after one of the parties is deceased. This would suggest that a friendship can be formed and maintained without the presumed necessity of shared spatial and temporal encounter, and without the conscious presence of the other. If this is so, then one can truly make friends with the dead. I have looked intimately through Wistrand's lens, and my meditation on his framing, cuts, jerks and pans have set the process of introjection in motion. The preceding writing could be read as the beginnings of a friendship between (or rather *within*) myself and Wistrand. Indeed, having engaged with his professional grievances, his misgivings as a father, his emotional need for remembrance, perhaps we are now on first name terms. According to his surviving family who I had some correspondence with, he liked to go by his middle name, Hugo. Let's momentarily suspend the paradoxes and aporias present in the assertion that I am friends with a dead man whom I have never met and ask, assuming that we are friends, what kind of friendship Hugo and I have.

Derrida locates the essence of friendship in the structure of surviving, which dictates that eventually one of you will die and the other will be left behind 'responsible and responsive to the intemporal, and largely irretrievable mute other' (Ronell 2006:30). As such, friendship opens up the experience of time and is for Derrida, as with Nietzsche, inflected with the future. My friendship with Hugo, both *like* the archive and *of* the archive, is a question of the future, a future for which, in this book, I am left responsible, through my citation and recitation of the departed diplomat. As the survivor of our proposed friendship, I feel bound by certain duties and taxes which must be paid to my departed other. Ronell feels similarly tied to Acker, asking 'Is there any discernible duty free zone in friendship? . . . The friend leaves you . . . with a number of pressing questions, a number of pressure points susceptible to unceasing pain' (2006:25-6). In the context of this chapter, I am left with the pressing question of Hugo's place in the events that occurred between Japan and China in 1937. It is Hugo's films that have afforded me the inspiration and opportunity to engage with these events, thereby making this project and, by extension, myself, gratefully indebted to him.

According to Derrida, thinking and thanking are inextricably linked—to think someone means that you thank them. As Ronell remarks, 'to the extent that I thank (think) you I am being called by you. The call comes from within me and beyond me' (2006:29). Ronell clarifies that within a good friendship, to think the other is to give them due thanks. But it does not seem enough thanks for me to simply *think* Hugo. To truly think someone you must have free rein to think whatever you like, however bad, however critical. This is the legacy implicit in Ronell and Acker's posthumous friendship, a friendship which dissolves the economy of give and take, yet maintains an ethical strain (2006:28). Conversely, I feel duty bound to repay Hugo for thinking him critically. Thinking him is not giving thanks within the structure of our relationship, rather I feel bound to give thanks, or perhaps even compensation, for having cited him in such critical terms. Unlike Ronell's citing of Acker, my citing of Hugo does not bond me to him, it binds me.

In thinking thanking I am brought back to the ethics of exchange and am reminded again by Derrida of the impossibility of a principle of reciprocity residing within a true gift. And for Derrida, as for Ronell, good friendship is a true gift in which principles of reciprocity are never present. Similarly, for Nietzsche friendship demands a rupture in equality, with good friendship being born of disproportion. Hugo's films, and his friendship, were never and will never be a true gift from him to me—how could they when they were never given? I did not receive these films as a gift from a friend but took them, and am exacting on them, and Hugo, a narcissistic reappropriation.

Split between two poles that do not form a polarity I am caught. Reflecting on Kathy Acker, on assignment, makes me examine the disjunction between *narcissism* (where I claim the friend as part of me) and *alterity* (I cannot appropriate the friend to myself or exercise a narcissistic reappropriation of sorts, operate a reduction of the friend to the same or to the friend as the other). . . . Sometimes I am seduced by the possibility of giving in to proximity—I have pulled Kathy in, close to me, and I want to accomplish the fusion of you and me. But then I remember Nietzsche's lessons, the call to maintain or keep a relentless distance within a good friendship.
(Ronell 2006:27)

Being (for the most part) a good friend to Kathy by maintaining the proper degree of noble Nietzschean distance, Ronell expresses uneasiness at writing in the first person ('saying, for me, brazenly, "I" makes me shudder' (2006:26)). I find it almost impossible to do anything but include myself in the first person when writing on Hugo.

For all its dumb and numb lethargy, the university issued a menace to her exercise of linguistic promiscuity, threatening at every turn to revoke her poetic license; it put her in a libidinal straight jacket, calmed her roguish stories—wait a minute, I may be mixing us up here and talking about my...
(Ronell 2006:15)

                                                              self.

Including myself in his narrative, sometimes crudely, is my way of attempting a fair exchange with Hugo. I feel that if I am to air his dirty laundry for all to see, then I had better offer some of my own private filth, something perversely personal, in return. As I have made and kept my friendship with Hugo out of duty, bound by reciprocal laws, it does not qualify as a good friendship. Not wanting to be thought of as a bad friend leads me to search for some other title I can project onto my relationship with Theodor Hugo Wistrand. To avoid committing myself to any prescribed codes of conduct (or conduction), I will snatch at a conveniently ill-defined title that I can reappropriate. If Wistrand and I do not have a friendship then perhaps we have a *necromance*. Yes, it is romance of sorts, an intemporal date with a dead man. And because we are in a bargaining relationship, a semi-professional exchange, my (nec)romancing of Wistrand has an air of prostitution about it. Perhaps in the sense that, like Ronell, I am always on call to my departed other, to Wistrand, I am his call girl, trading in secret information. First, Wistrand and I politely converse with each other, jumping through the hoops of small talk. Then we move onto a discussion of his professional life, coaxing out the secrets, testing how much each of us is prepared to give. Eventually we tentatively tackle each other's personal lives, weighing up the anecdotes and stories, trying to attain equal levels of intimacy. Under the rules of this necromance, I am bound to give some tit for his tat, to be the Kleinian 'good breast', a title Ronell bestows upon Acker who, she recalls, regularly gave her hats as gifts and who 'like all good breasts . . . invites ambivalence and poisoning, a reflex of destruction' (2006:24).

> The boy was so shocked at the blood bath he had witnessed that he ran off to the other caravan and said nothing. Being even more shocked at the painless excretion of blood which continued to pour from her, Scarlett sat on the toilet and kept still, listening to the red flow fall into the water. Half an hour or so must have gone by before Sadie and Lisa became concerned by the boy's silence and pallor, and came back to the caravan to check on her. The front door was locked and she would not move from the bathroom, so

they had to climb in through the window to get in. Sadie had the sense to call for an ambulance which, on the Isle of Cumbrae, was a police van driven by a solitary young copper who looked little older than them. The uniformed lad asked Scarlett how much she was bleeding. She didn't know how to answer, she didn't know what measure of blood loss he expected her to answer through. Much more than a period but less than a gunshot wound? Scarlett said nothing. 'She's bleeding a lot,' Sadie answered for her, 'it's all over her skirt'. The copper gave her a plastic bin liner to sit on, so that she would not get blood on the seat of his van.

One historian estimated that if the dead of Nanking were to link hands, they would stretch from Nanking to the city of Hangchow, spanning a distance of some two hundred miles. Their blood would weigh twelve hundred tons, and their bodies would fill twenty-five railroad cars. Stacked on top of each other, these bodies would reach the height of a seventy-four-story building.
(Chang 1997:5)

How can one test the levels of something for which there is no unit of measure? What kind of scale compares the weight of two beauties, the gravity of duties, or the ground speed of joy? What kind of gauge can quantify intimacy, rage, narratives, passion, secrets, violence, love, or the depths of red? In trying to measure tit for tat, what kind of equation can I possibly employ? Ronell states that 'Kathy had ways of testing your friendship' (1996:20), but does not tell us how her tests were carried out, or the results measured. Perhaps this is because—as Ronell tells us in *The Test Drive* (2005) which, while a work in progress, she discussed at length with Kathy—knowing you are being tested may collapse the premises of the test. In 'Kathy Goes To Hell', Ronell writes:

> The modality of the test interested me in light of a chapter I was completing entitled "Testing Your Friendship". The test of friendship that I overtly explore is organized around the break up of Nietzsche and Wagner, which Heidegger sees as a historical event, involving the end of metaphysics—involving, in other words, the very way in which we think and make love (2006:20).

Curiously, this quote contains two misnomers, as if Ronell had left them there to test the reader, who might also be her friend. Firstly, *The Test Drive* is not divided into chapters, but parts. This alone could be a minor semantic slip-up which Ronell simply overlooked. The second misnomer seems more deliberate, however. The *part* organized around the breakup of Nietzsche and Wagner is not entitled 'Testing Your Friendship'—there is no such part or subheading in the book—it is entitled 'Testing Your Love, or: Breaking Up'. If this were a Freudian slip, what might have prompted Ronell to make it? Perhaps she projects the split in her relationship with Acker onto Nietzsche and Wagner's break up and, in so doing, finds it too painful to write a word as strong as 'love' in reference to the (two) pair(s), so seeks emotional refuge under the duller title of 'friendship'. If it is a deliberate mistake left there to test the reader, then for what purpose are we being tested, and how will she ever know who passed?

In her essay on Kathy, Ronell mentions that to describe tests and testability, the Greeks used the word *basanos*, which is linked to torture (2006:20). In Part 2 of *The Test Drive* she elaborates that in Athenian society, the slave body was emblematic of the practice of torture and testing, and that it was thought that through torture/testing, a latent truth could be brought to light. It is from this forgotten source that the current Western usages of testing were first imprinted. So genealogically speaking, testing implies a form of bodily pain, or threat of pain, akin to torture, and contemporarily speaking, it demands that the test subject must not know they are being tested.

> Scarlett was driven to the local nurses' station as there was no hospital on the island. In this Dickensian institution, two nurses told her (in a tone that implied 'we see little sluts like you all the time, so what are you making such a fuss about?') not to worry as she was 'just having a little miscarriage'. Scarlett knew that this was not, and could not be, the case. They insisted they knew best and gave her an ultrasound scan to test her claim. On finding an empty womb, the

nurses called on a retired local doctor to investigate. Clearly disgruntled at having been woken at 2am, the doctor barked at the nurses about Scarlett, and never spoke to her. Up until this point, the experience had been shocking and dizzying, but painless. Having bound her legs into stirrups the doctor used a metal clamp to keep Scarlett open and used every available tool to test for the cause of the bleeding. Now she wished that Sadie was there holding her hand, like she would have been the year before, but she was sitting with Lisa in the corridor outside the room, probably wondering why Scarlett always had to be 'different'. The two nurses had also left the room at this point, leaving Scarlett alone with old doctor. He then began exacting on her what felt like purposeful acts of torture while she screamed in pain, begging for him to stop. He did not stop until he was good and ready, and until every shiny tool in the place was covered with her blood.

What would be a concept of equality, an equity, which would no longer be calculated according to our systems of equivalence? Or a political structure that would no longer inscribe a movement beyond proportion or approportion, exceeding thereby all love of the proper? Traditionally, friendship has

modelled politics, which is why they are often anamorphic of one another, mirroring and distorting, calling the other to order, working without respite on justice and the possibility of being a good friend . . . The friend, in one sense, has not arrived, even after her departure. Perhaps the same can be said for democracy or the historical experience of justice.
(Ronell 2006:29)

Mimicking Ronell's oscillation between the classical and the contemporary, between the private and the public, friendship and politics, I return to the events of 1937. I return to red, to death, torture, blood, body counts, latent truths, the historical experience of justice, and Wistrand who, as any test would prove, is not my friend. Like myself and Wistrand, Japan and the US have always lacked a good friendship, even when allied. The Hanami for cherry blossom trees filmed by Wistrand is also celebrated in Washington DC, to celebrate the giving of two Japanese cherry trees by the mayor of Tokyo to the city of Washington. These were ceremonially planted in West Potomac Park in Washington by the First Lady and the wife of the Japanese ambassador. The gift was not a true one or, at least, the US government did not respond to it as such. By 1915 the US government reciprocated by giving flowering dogwood trees to the people of Japan. In 1927 a group of American school children re-enacted the planting of the cherry trees in Washington, and by 1935, this had developed into the National Cherry

Blossom Festival. This supposed display of friendship was quashed during WWII when Japan and the US fell out, or broke up, and was resumed in 1947 when they again became allied. If the gift is a test of friendship, then it is in the absence of an obligation to reciprocate that a pair pass, and in the presence of it that they fail.

The experimental disposition of humanity proposed by Nietzsche, which Ronell takes as her starting point in *The Test Drive,* is perhaps exaggerated during times of war, when what is staked on particular tests, or tortures, is raised to a matter of life and death. There were a number of occurrences at Nanking which might be understood retrospectively as manifestations of such tests (and here I will not go into the tests to which the people of Nanking were subjected after the massacre, in the form of medical experiments from 1939 until the Japanese surrendered in 1945). The foreign diplomats and journalists posted in Nanking were offered escape prior to the Japanese invasion of the city via the *Panay*, a ship that had been granted diplomatic immunity by the Japanese to transport foreigners out of China. It would embark from the Nanking port on the Yangtze river. Most of the foreign diplomats and journalists chose to take this escape route, but a few stayed against their countries' orders in the hope that they might be able to assist the Chinese in Nanking after the Japanese had invaded by maintaining an International Safety Zone within the city. What they did not know was that this would become a test of courage and resolve on which their bodily safety depended.

On 12th December 1937, three days after it had left the banks of Nanking, Japanese aviators bombed and machine gunned the *Panay*, resulting in two fatalities and a great number of injured passengers. As it turned out, Nanking was actually a safer place to be than the ship that offered an escape from it. The reasons behind the assault on the *Panay* remain unclear. At the time the Japanese claimed that it was a mistake made by confused aviators in the heat of battle, and that fog or smoke prevented them from seeing the American flags on the ship. However, the bombing happened on a clear day. Furthermore, the US had cracked the Japanese military code, which they dubbed code RED (really), so knew that the aviators had received explicit orders to bomb the *Panay*. According to Chang's account, there may have been a second test manifest in this event. She surmises that the bombing of the *Panay* may have been a test on the part of the Japanese to see how the Americans would react.

In this instance, for the US government, RED was both the bearer and repressor of sensitive political and military information. In part because they did not want to expose their cracking of code RED (which also gave them knowledge of the intentions of the Japanese government to stonewall foreign diplomats from Nanking in case they relayed to their home countries unfavourable reports on the military's activities), the American government had to play along with the explanation of accidental attack given by Japan. This was made especially difficult by the footage of the sinking of the *Panay* shot by two American news reporters, Norman Alley and Eric Mayell of Fox Movietone. Alley and Mayell had been on board the *Panay* and shot 5,300-foot rolls of film of the attack. The two hid with the other passengers under the river bank reeds following the assault, and protected the film by wrapping it in canvas and burying it in the mud. When the footage was later unearthed and shipped to the US, President Roosevelt requested that they cut thirty feet of the footage before showing it in movie theatres. The thirty feet to be erased from public view revealed several Japanese gunmen shooting at the ship from nearly deck level, and would have made a case of mistaken identity impossible to maintain. In his book *The Panay Incident* (1969), Hamilton Darby Parry suggests that the US government was anxious to reach a diplomatic and financial settlement with Japan, which would have been made impossible if it were public knowledge that the *Panay* was attacked deliberately. The US exhibited a tactical response (of erasure and repression) to a testing situation. (This response to the atrocities related to Nanking are preminiscent of a later filmic erasure. In 1988, the Shochiku Fuji Distribution Company enraged Bernardo Bertolucci by clandestinely removing a thirty-second sequence from *The Last Emperor* before its Japanese release. The removed sequence contained the only depiction of the Rape of Nanking, and its censoring was termed 'revolting' by Bertolucci, and a 'mutilation' of his film (Chang 1997:210).)

Of the few foreigners who passed the test and stayed in Nanking to maintain the International Safety Zone, two in particular stand out—both have books published posthumously on their actions, and feature heavily in Chang's account. Minnie Vautrin and John Rabe were respectively dubbed 'the American Goddess' and 'the living Buddha' of Nanking. Minnie Vautrin was the head of the Education Department and dean of studies at Ginling Arts and

Science College in Nanking, which became integral part of the International Safety Zone, housing ten thousand Chinese civilians at the massacre's height. As the most senior member of the school present, Vautrin also became the head of the International Safety Zone, negotiating with Japanese soldiers in an attempt to prevent, or at least minimize, their rape of Chinese women. Preminiscent of the work of many present-day western do-gooders, Vautrin's efforts were not always successful, and were often misplaced. Vautrin regularly ran to the areas of the Safety Zone which she heard had been infiltrated by Japanese soldiers, in response to reports of the rape of children, the elderly, and pregnant women. Most often arriving too late to intervene, Vautrin agreed to the request of a high-ranking Japanese officer that, in exchange for leaving the 'respectable' women alone, they would be allowed into the Safety Zone to pick out a hundred prostitute women among the ten thousand refugees, and take them to the local comfort house. How the officers were able to distinguish the 'prostitute' women from the 'respectable' ones is unclear, but they only succeeded in finding twenty-one. Vautrin's gift of 'prostitutes' was not reciprocated. After the twenty-one women were removed, the Japanese soldiers continued covert raids of the Safety Zone, often coaxing Vautrin out of Ginling College under false pretences in order to do so. Chang heralds Vautrin the 'living goddess' and heroine of the massacre, yet it seems to me that she maintained a perhaps naively optimistic stance, telling the refugees that as China would no doubt triumph over Japan, they should maintain overt national pride.

The second western 'hero' who refused to board the *Panay* was businessman John Rabe. Rabe was an unlikely candidate for helping the Chinese, being German (Germany was allied with Japan) and the leader of the Nazi party in Nanking. However, when donning his Nazi armband, Rabe was able to forthrightly order soldiers off their Chinese victims—such was the Party's sway with Japan. By all accounts, it seems that Rabe's swastika acted as a potent symbol not of genocide, but of protection—less akin to the Third Reich than to the charitable Buddhist organization known as the Red Swastika Society whom he witnessed pulling bodies from ponds filled with blood. And in a sense, Rabe's swastika did metamorphosise into a respectable red when, in April 1938, he was awarded the Service Cross of the Red Cross Order for his peace-keeping actions in Nanking.

There were girls under the age of 8 and women over the age of 70 who were raped and then, in the most brutal way possible, knocked down and beat up. We found corpses of women on beer glasses and others who had been lanced by bamboo shoots. I saw the victims with my own eyes—I talked to some of them right before their deaths. . . .
Rabe's Report to Hitler (1938)

On becoming aware of the violence likely to be perpetrated on Nanking, Rabe wired Hitler on 25th November 1937, and later Kreibel, asking for help. Neither replied. Between December 1937 and April 1938, Rabe made several attempts to communicate the atrocities at Nanking to his leaders, in order that they might use their political influence with Japan to stop the violence. (Apparently Rabe was blissfully unaware of the unforgotten holocaust swelling in his own country.) Rabe obtained a copy of the only footage of the Nanking Massacre and took this with him to Germany where he arrived in April 1938. The film was shot by another Zone leader, John Magee, and made it out of Nanking and to Germany and the US, on the person of YMCA administrator, George Fitch, who stitched the negatives into the lining of his camel hair coat before he left the city. Rabe immediately began trying to publicize the massacre around Berlin, showing the film and lecturing on it at the War Ministry, Siemans Company, Association for the Far East and Ministry of Foreign Affairs. Despite his efforts, Rabe failed to meet with Hitler on his return to Berlin, so instead sent him a copy of the film along with a written report on the events in Nanking. It is unknown whether Hitler saw the film or read the report, but following Rabe's publicity frenzy, he was warned by the Gestapo never to lecture on or discuss the occurrences in Nanking again, and was told that his findings would not affect Germany's foreign policy towards Japan.

So, the friendship between Japan and Nazi Germany was maintained. It passed this test of exposure, and stood stalwart in the light of Magee's film and Rabe's written account. But the exposure split the friendship between the Nazi command and Rabe who, in 1946 was finally de-nazified by the de-nazifying commission of the British sector in Charlottenberg. In a 1945 diary entry Rabe writes, 'If I had known of any atrocities of the Nazis in China I wouldn't have entered the NSDAP', and following his de-nazification that 'the nerve torture finally came to an end'. Nonetheless, Rabe's benevolent acts in China were ignored in Europe, and he was condemned to a life of hardship and unemployment because of his prior relationship with the Nazi Party. Rabe's was a test in which the historical experience of justice, like the friend, had not arrived even after its departure.

The victims of the Nanking Massacre and their families were subject to a similar historical experience of (in)justice. In its effort to form an alliance with Japan, the government of the People's Republic of China announced that it forgave Japan for its actions during WWII and to prove this, invited the Japanese prime minister to visit mainland China in 1991. According to Chang's interviews with victims of the Nanking Massacre, these announcements, made without the receipt of an official apology from Japan, felt like 'a second rape'. Because of the attempt by China and Japan to strike-up a new friendship, an experience of justice has never arrived to the victims of Nanking, as through their government's forgiveness, the need for justice has supposedly already departed. The survivors of the Nanking Massacre and their families feel they are victims of a historical injustice, and await apology and compensation. I wonder though, how the sincerity of an apology or an amount of compensation, can be measured and deemed justly equivalent to an experience in history like the Nanking Massacre. Twenty-four million dollars for twelve hundred tonnes of blood, an apology said in a sombre tone at an international summit for twenty-five railroad cars filled with dead bodies, or a trust fund set up for every relative of the corpses piled to the height of a seventy-four storey building?

Once he had finished conducting his tests on her, the doctor claimed that Scarlett was 'fixed' for now. He then called in the nurses who helped him plug her up with gauze, and she was sent over by ambulance on the car ferry to the hospital in Glasgow. Here her treatment was far more humane. They told her that she had sustained a high vaginal laceration and was haemorrhaging as a result. For now, they said, all that could be done was to put pressure on the tear by packing Scarlett with gauze until the bleeding stopped. But they would not, or could not, explain to her why the doctor on Cumbrae did the torturous things he did to her cunt before inserting the gauze. For a long time after, she felt she was to blame for what happened, that the bleeding and the torture was punishment for being pompous or screwed up enough to claim that she was more akin to a contemporary's mother than lover. She felt that it was self-inflicted, a kind of suicide. Fucking suicide.

Much of what Kathy had to say was prophetic, hence her particular brand of irony. In the same novel [*My Mother: Demonology, A Novel*], she opens a section called "Dreaming Politics" with these questions: "Where does Bush's power stop? Where does an authoritarian leader's power stop? Tell me, Mommy, where and how will Bush's power stop?" She saw the terrifying lineage, the future history of spilt blood.

. . . Oh, the history of blood. I forgot to say that the book cover is bright red. Yes, red. Here's another red thread I would have wanted to follow (I cannot stop reading Kathy, finding it impossible to let go, to end).
(Ronell 2006:32)

Whatever tests might be adopted to weigh up the blood lost during the Nanking Massacre, it is clear that a sizeable portion of it was spilt as the result of suicides. The duties of a Japanese soldier went way beyond the usual demands of military service. 'So harsh was [the Japanese] code,' writes Chang, 'that its most notable characteristic was the moral imperative that adherents commit suicide if they ever failed to meet honourably the obligations of military service—often with the highly ceremonial and extremely painful ritual of hari-kiri, in which the warrior met death by unflinchingly disembowelling himself in front of witnesses' (Chang 1997:20). Indeed, in Japanese military school, the pressure to do well was such that exam results were kept secret from the students to minimize the risk of suicide as a response to failure. Whilst the suicides of the Japanese were most often confined to the (male) military, suicides in the Chinese population as a response to military activities (in Nanking in particular) were most common among women. Chinese women who were raped and became pregnant by Japanese soldiers often could not face either having the child or committing infanticide. As a result, between 1937 and 1938, Chang tells us, 'a German diplomat reported that "uncounted" Chinese women were taking their own lives by flinging themselves into the Yangtze River' (1997:90).

Wherever she is, ahead of me or behind me,
I expect the friend; I am pregnant with her. I
carry her for an interminable term.
(Ronell 2006:29)

Ronell feels that she and Kathy should have both disappeared at the same time. She recalls the sentiments of a Deleuzian friend of hers who once said, following the Jonestown mass suicides, that 'there exists a strong desire in us for synchronicity in death, a wish that we all die at the same moment' (2006:18). The ego would like that there was neither one of us left weeping, inconsolable and alone, nor one having to think that the world would continue in her absence. For a friend, or channel, the painful solitude of loss might prompt the desire to end one's own life, to enter into the inconceivable abyss that appears, in life, to be inhabited by one's departed others. This seems to have been the case for Vautrin who, by surviving the Nanking Massacre, survived the countless Chinese women whom she had befriended, the women who, during the massacre, took their own lives or had their lives taken. On 14th May 1940, Vautrin returned to the US from Nanking, feeling she was unable to cope in the aftermath of the massacre. She suffered a breakdown as a result, but by April 1941 she appeared to be making a recovery, prompting a psychiatrist to recommend that she not be institutionalised but instead stay with friends. It must, therefore, have come as a shock to them that, on 14th May 1941, Vautrin killed herself while alone in the apartment of her friend (a secretary of the United Christian Missionary Society) by opening the gas jet on the kitchen stove (Hua-Ling 2000:143-4). On the point of Vautrin's death, Chang's transmission of her departed heroine runs somewhat awry. Chang mistakenly writes in her account of Vautrin's suicide that, rather than it occurring in the apartment of the friend with whom she was staying, which by all other accounts is accurate, 'Vautrin sealed the windows and doors of *her [own] home* . . . , turned on the gas, and committed suicide' (Chang 1997:187 emphasis added). Chang's inattention to the details of Vautrin's suicide is perhaps symptomatic of her preoccupying wish to introject, or narcissistically reappropriate Minnie to the same, to herself. Chang would have liked to have been a 'goddess' of Nanking, and perhaps through her channelling and resurrection of the ghosts of the massacre, she was. Like Vautrin, however, Chang found the burden of the massacre's aftermath, the closeness to so many tortured deaths, too much to survive. Chang had suffered from clinical depression for the years after writing *The Rape of Nanking* and was institutionalized as a result. In June 2004, however, she appeared to be making a recovery so was released. Like Vautrin's, Chang's 'recovery' proved to be false. Five months later, on 9th November 2004, Chang stopped her car on a rural road near her home in California and shot herself in the head (Sullivan 2004:b06). Her transmission, *The Rape of Nanking*, survives her. I forgot to say that the book cover is bright red. Yes, red. Here's another red thread I would have wanted to follow.

Ok, I finally know how I should have begun to write about Kathy. Now that I have reflected on her romanced red, it becomes clear to me. To do some justice to Kathy's thought, I should have begun with the utterance, signalled under a somewhat representational drawing, "my cunt red ugh". It's so obvious to me now. This is where she locates the matricial origin. Now when it has become too late, I understand where my friend and mistress would have wanted me to start, where I might have begun on the path of a worthy homage. Oh Kathy! It's all in this endless little phrase.
(Ronell 2006:33)

Chang's husband, brother, parents and son also survive her. What would it be like to survive a mother's suicide? Curiously, Ronell fails to mention that her friend Kathy knew the answer to this question. In 1977, when Acker was thirty years old, her mother killed herself. Might this be why it is in her 'cunt red ugh', in the maternal passage that is 'the colour of rage and violence' and in an utterance that is at once asignificatory and polysemic, that Kathy locates the matricial origin? These two red books, perhaps like Wistrand's red films, bear the future history of spilt blood, the mark of 'unspeakable evil', and their terrifying lineages seem to be carried on the X chromosome. The blood that has been spilt and the people who have split in the histories relayed in this chapter, are most often female. It is as though the colour red, and the suicide, decay and violence with which it is inflected, harks back to a maternal/matricial origin.

> The doctors and nurses at the hospital in Glasgow wanted to call Scarlett's mother to tell her what was happening with her daughter's cunt. It being Scarlett's first holiday without parental supervision, she preferred that her mother remain unworried, in blissful ignorance until she returned home to London, recovered. Because she was sixteen the hospital could not legally inform Scarlett's parents of her medical situation without her consent. Then, in what seemed to Scarlett an act of extreme selfishness, Sadie split on her. She and Lisa did not stay with Scarlett in the hospital. They left by ferry to Cumbrae to return to their 'bad boys' in the caravan park less than two hours after arriving in Glasgow. They left Scarlett alone and mute among medical staff who seemed fascinated by her genitalia. Countless trainee doctors asked her if she minded them having a look at her laceration, at the little tear that was all the way up there.

Scarlett obliged. She became accustomed to spreading her legs for anyone wearing a badge. It became their cunt, their little specimen, their prime example of an anomaly. I say 'anomaly' because nobody could explain how the laceration, the root of the bleeding, had been made, including to their frustration, Scarlett. 'It could only have been caused by a sharp object being inserted into the vagina,' they kept telling her, waiting for a confession. She had nothing more to confess. 'We had some regular teenage fumbling, we nearly had sex but we didn't. Nothing kinky happened.' She almost wished it had. They never believed Scarlett's story. They sent in an over-zealous social worker to interrogate her. 'Did he have a knife?' she asked, 'did he have a piece of wire?' No! She got no more out of Scarlett than the rest of the staff who treated her as though she were a poor, passive, abused girl. Scarlett felt this might be her fault for having taken up a maternal stance that refused the boy, for having been a bad breast.

Despite her attention to red, to Kathy's red cunt, and to loss, Acker's maternal origin is something Ronell almost ignores, allowing her train of thought to be interrupted by other voices, paternal ones in particular. Rather than starting with the matricial origin, with 'my cunt red ugh', as she should have, Ronell begins with a paternal origin, weaving Derridaddy into her homage to Acker from the outset. Ronell's bracketed tale of Derrida and Acker, which fills the first two pages of 'Kathy Goes to Hell', is introduced as her having begun 'by backing up, returning to an ostensible starting point, a point of entry' (2006:12). Derridaddy, not Kathy, is Ronell's starting point, the one to whom she ceaselessly returns, for whom the lines are always open, and with whom there can be no splits. Ronell tells us how she used to accompany Derrida (who would always arrive 'early, very early') to the airport and wait with him for his flight to depart at the Air France terminal. Again playing the handmaid (who, for Margaret Atwood, is always shrouded in red), Ronell has 'a thing' about getting her friends to meet in a calculable way, and to 'cross one another's paths - or pathologies, depending on what configuration of encounter seems more improbable. It's the perv in me, or the hysteric, who likes to stir trouble' (2006:12). As a manifestation of this perversion, or hysteria, Ronell would regularly bring along one of her friends as a 'show and tell' while she waited with Derrida at the airport (2006:13). About two years before Acker's death, she introduced Derridaddy and Kathy at the Air France terminal. . . . Unfortunately the story ends there and the reader is left to guess what occurred when the father of deconstruction and the mother of punk literature crossed paths and pathologies. Speaking of pathologies, Derrida did share with Acker a demonstrable screw-up pertaining to the desire of his mother to kill herself. He expresses this in *Jacques Derrida, Circumfession* (1993), a book written with Geoffrey Bennington, in which Bennington sets out to write a systematic account of Derrida's work (the section entitled *Jacques Derrida*), and Derrida responds with his most autobiographical utterances published under the title *Circumfession*, which is presented as a set of rogue footnotes at the bottom of each page of Bennington's more formal text. This book was published in English in 1993, the same year Acker published on her 'cunt red ugh' in *My Mother: Demonology, A Novel*. Despite both texts being dislikeable in many ways and narcissistically charged, I cannot help being necromantically attracted to their authors and wanting to hook them up. Ronell also omits this connection between her two friends. So I am calling on Derrida's ghost again, and will let his voice run to the end of this section, taking us back to film and through film, to the root of all this red.

> 1. The crude word, fight with him in this way over what's crude, as though first of all I liked to raise the stakes, and the expression "raise the stakes" is one that belongs to my mother, as though I were attached to him so as to look for a fight over what talking crude means, as though I were trying relentlessly, to the point of bloodshed, to remind him [...]

> 7. .... among other remorses with respect to my mother, [I] feel really guilty for publishing her end, in exhibiting her last breaths and, still worse, for purposes that some might judge as to be literary, at risk of

adding a dubious exercise to the "writer and his mother" series, subseries "the mother's death" . . . I remember that December 24, 1988, when already she was hardly saying anything articulate anymore, nor apparently fitting the situation, nothing that thus seemed to answer to the normal rule of human exchange, she pronounced clearly, in the midst of confused groanings "I want to kill myself". . . . "I want to kill myself" is a sentence of mine, me all over, but known to me alone, the mise en scène of a suicide and the fictive but oh how motivated, convinced, serious decision to put an end to my days, a decision constantly relaunched, a rehearsal which occupies the entire time of my internal theatre, the show I put on before myself without a break, before a crowd of ghosts. . . . (1993:37)

> The next day the bleeding still had not stopped. 'We might need to take you into theatre,' they said (she pictured red velvet curtains spreading to reveal a black backdropped stage), 'we might need to stitch you under general anaesthetic; there is always a risk that you will die under general anaesthetic, you might want your mother there.' On fantasising the audible tears that she expected to be spilt in the event of her

bloody death, Scarlett succumbed and gave them permission to call her mother, who was always on call to her. Following the phone call, Mother made it by plane from London to the hospital in Glasgow in 8 hours. Scarlett doesn't remember her arriving. What she does remember is Mother's refrain, her attempt to displace Scarlett's attention from her cunt (and now I notice how every time I write the word 'cunt' my computer underlines it in red). Mother kept looking out of the hospital ward's window onto the car park and commenting on how many red cars there were. 'Why are there so many red cars here?', she would ask. Again, Scarlett had no answer.

. . . the incessant return of the "I want to kill myself" speaks less the desire to put an end to my life than a sort of compulsion to overtake each second, like one car overtaking another, doubling it rather, overprinting it with the negative of a photograph already taken with a "delay" mechanism, the memory of what survived me to be present at my disappearance, interprets or runs the film again. . . .
(Derrida 1993:36-9)

At the beginning of this chapter I made the point that channels are active agents who, like mediums, are never neutral. If I am Wistrand's channel, I can only be so secondarily, through the celluloid which is his primary medium. Wistrand's film, or rather, the film onto which Wistrand recorded images, has silently acted as the driving force behind the spliterature that has emerged in this chapter. Like a red car speeding past a hearse, Wistrand's films have overtaken him, doubling their meaning. And it is in the film's agency, its turn to red, that the split between the celluloid and the diplomat is manifest.

Ugh! Now it dawns on me, the way you
pull away from your own boldness, you
avert your gaze with a grunt—is it guttural
or soft, maybe hoarse? I am trying to hear
you—in this nearly visceral moment, your
sigh and your sign, the way you pull away,
the distress held in an autocratic sputter.
Ugh. . . . Your unbearable red cunt: how you
were and weren't re(a)d.
(Ronell 2006:33)

Like Ronell's return to Kathy's endless 'my cunt red ugh' that might mark Acker's split from her mother, the film's turn to red is an endless little visual phrase that marks its split from Wistrand. Each time the celluloid is played its redness has increased. This form of 'decay' is neither self-destructive nor suicidal, rather, it is indicative of the film's vitality, of a living memory working in opposition to Wistrand's. The film survives Wistrand happily. Each time the film is played and is re(a)d again, it usurps Wistrand, tempting me away from him with its affective or visceral pull. Red is the silent 'ugh' of the film, the asignificatory and polysemic utterance of one who both recalls and supersedes its maker. The film has broken up with the filmmaker, it takes autocracy for a test drive, and implores me to do the same.

Epilogue
January 2021

It was a Friday morning when I received the email from Fran with the 'Seeing Red, Hearing the Dead' chapter attached. Ahead of me was a full day of online sessions, which I find more tiring than in-person sessions because of the extra effort it takes to make and sustain a connection with patients. It is as though the screen absorbs the unconscious communication that would pass between us more easily in the room, like a sponge providing unwanted sound-proofing against emotional noise.

Just after 8:00 p.m. I poured a large whiskey and prepared myself to open the chapter. I was filled with the same sense of dread I had on discovering the first set of emails Scarlett sent. Then I had berated myself for not checking the inbox and failing to respond to the years of unread messages from Scarlett, but also for some of the content of the responses I had sent while she was in DC. It was uncomfortable to read some of my interpretations, especially the ones that seemed to suggest that her (homo)sexuality was a sign of narcissism. I noticed that I entirely overlooked Scarlett's questioning of what her gendered position could be within a binary structure, despite her explicitly expressing her discomfort with it. There it was in black and white; like the majority of my colleagues in the 1990s, I had been behind the times, and upheld a heterosexual ideal to the detriment of a gay patient. If I could travel back in time and respond to Scarlett's emails with the affirmative approach I take now, I wonder whether the outcome of the therapy, and of Scarlett's life and death, might have been different. But there was now the possibility of making reparation, and I was determined to provide something helpful to Scarlett's surviving family.

As I read the chapter Fran sent it became clear that my renewed dread was warranted. I could feel Scarlett's slipping into psychosis, her symbolic equation, her falling into bed with the dead. And yet Fran's desperation was palpable, her need for me to provide some reassurance that the accident was not Scarlett's fault, that her life-partner did not leave her, and their children, intentionally. I scrambled among Scarlett's schizophrenic voices, maternal suicides, test drives, death drives, splits and red cunts to try to find a conclusively healthy and hopeful interpretation I could offer back to Fran. Every avenue I pursued turned in on itself with a double-bind, each point that implied a life force was laced with a corresponding death drive. Scarlett might have termed this simultaneous urge to maintain and to destroy an 'archive fever'. Was it death by archive fever? Perhaps. But this sketchy formulation would not be helpful to Fran and the twins.

As I mulled all this it also occurred to me that I have become the sole container of portions of Scarlett's archive.

There is the portion that, unusually for private therapy, is documented in writing, in Scarlett's inbox and in mine. But there is a further portion of Scarlett's archive, our in-person sessions, that are held solely within my mind. My memory is the abode in which the thoughts and feelings Scarlett brought to therapy in the late 1990s are stored, and where they remain, gradually decaying, without public access. Indeed, the necessity of confidentiality in my profession means that this portion of any patient's archive is restricted even to their next of kin. This has proved a most frustrating and painful fact for Fran. I could not offer her comfort by allowing her access to these necessarily restricted areas of Scarlett's archive, as she would have liked me to, but I wanted to be able to soothe her in some way, to offer her some sort of solace.

In the hope of finding something with a clearer meaning, another email from Scarlett I had missed, perhaps, I returned to my forgotten inbox. I remembered Scarlett's hopeful checking of her spam to see whether she had missed a reply from me. I decided to do the same, entering Scarlett's name into the search box for the spam folder, rather than the inbox. A single, bold, unread message was returned, a beacon of hope. The email was subject-headed 'Monologue with Derrida' and contained no message in the body of the email, just an attachment of the same name. I felt relieved until I absorbed the meaning of the time and date it arrived: 2:00 a.m. on 26/09/2011—several hours after Scarlett's accident on the night of the 25th. My hand began to shake, my throat tightened, I gripped the edge of my desk as though it would somehow protect me from the potential horror that lay ahead. Was this a message that outlived its moment of recording? Was it sent after the death of its sender intentionally, as some sort of suicide note or morbid trick? I paused, poured the whiskey from my glass back into the bottle (I would need a clear head for this), inhaled purposefully, willing myself calm, and opened the attachment. These, I believe, are Scarlett's last words.

Hannah Kublitz
29th January 2021

Monologue with Derrida

Let me speak, then, and find relief.
Job 31:20

Dear Professor Derrida,

Your writing on the archive has directed me to Yerushalmi's final chapter, his 'Monologue with Freud', that begins with the above quote from the book of Job, concludes his *Freud's Moses*, and contains, according to you, 'the umbilical cord of the book' (1995:37). By leading me in this way, I feel you have invited me to speak to you directly, as Yerushalmi did to Freud. If I have misheard you, if I have taken false dictation, I apologize, but this is a monologue and you will not interrupt me. In the words of Yerushalmi, Freud's posthumous son, his murdering Oedipus, 'I feel an inner need to speak to you and to have the audience eavesdrop, as it were' (1991:81).

I wish to ask you about the third and final thesis of *Archive Fever*, which you title '*3. Third Thesis and third* surenchère *(higher bid)*' (1995:95). This follows your first and second short theses, which are also titled first and second theses, and first and second higher bid respectively. In your final thesis and highest bid, which is only half a page in length, you are writing on the last lines of Yerushalmi's book and, by the closing line, on Anna Freud. I should back up here and, for the eavesdropping audience, say something more on Yerushalmi's monologue.

The last four paragraphs of Yerushalmi's letter to Freud, which concludes his book, are explicitly concerned with whether or not Freud believed psychoanalysis to be a Jewish science: 'I only want to know whether *you* ultimately came to believe it to be so', writes Yerushalmi (1991:100). The monologue's finale is also concerned, though secondarily, with Anna Freud's presence, or absence, at the International Association of Psychoanalysis's Congress in Jerusalem in 1977. Anna Freud was invited to give a paper at this event but was unable to make it. Instead, she sent a paper, or an inverted dictation, which was read aloud, on her behalf, to the assembled analysts. In his letter to her father, Yerushalmi writes that after Anna Freud's '. . . eminently suitable paper for the academic event, it was the abrupt and unexpected ending, in total discontinuity with what had come before, that sent a shock of amazement through the eminent audience' (1991:99).

In the unexpected ending Yerushalmi refers to, Anna Freud lists the criticisms to which psychoanalysis has been subject; 'for its methods being imprecise, its findings not open to proof by experiment, for being unscientific, even for being a "Jewish science"'. (As an aside, Professor, dare I say that Deconstruction could be equally subject to those criticisms?) The 'shocking' final line reads: 'However the other derogatory comments may be evaluated, it is, I believe, the last-mentioned connotation which, under present circumstances, can serve as a title of honour' (1977/1991:100). Yerushalmi asks whether this line may have been 'merely a rhetorical flourish' or meant contextually; that 'a "Jewish Science" is a title of honour for psychoanalysis in Jerusalem but not elsewhere' (1991: 100). Despite these two more likely hypotheses, Yerushalmi wishes it to have been a message from the spectre of Freud; a ghost speaking through his daughter's haunted writing and through the voice of the analyst designated to read the paper aloud. Yerushalmi further refines his question of the dead arch-patriarch, and his book concludes thus:

> I will . . . be content if you answer only one question: When your daughter conveyed these words to the congress in Jerusalem, was she speaking in your name? Please tell me, Professor, I promise I won't reveal your answer to anyone. (1991:100)

You have already said of this monologue, which ends with a whispered wish, that 'it does not say the truth it *makes* the truth' (1995:59). By this I think you mean that irrespective of whether or not Freud considered psychoanalysis to be a Jewish science, it becomes so through Yerushalmi's careful conjuring. In particular, you are saying that Yerushalmi speaks it into being when he addresses the dead arch-patriarch in the second person, and most significantly, when he does so under the covenant of 'we'. As you say in your *Foreword* 'We [Jews]' is a covenant to which, as a newborn at the point of his circumcision, and as a phantom at the point of Yerushalmi's address, Freud can only say 'yes' (1995:41).

What I wish to ask you about is your claim in the final subsection of your 'Theses' chapter titled '*3. Third Thesis and third* surenchère *(higher bid)*', that the archontic (by which you mean the laws of consignation and enclosure which are the very structure of the archive) is intrinsically, and exclusively, patriarchal. Allow me to quote a portion of your highest bid here:

> No one has analyzed, that is to say, deconstructed, the authority of the archontic principle better than [Freud]. No one has shown how this archontic, that is, paternal and patriarchic principle, only posited itself to repeat itself and returned to reposit itself only in parricide. . . . The equality and liberty of brothers. (1995: 95)

That the archive of Professor Mead, the 'grandmother to the world' has been debunked by a man would seem to support your claim that only brothers are equal and at liberty to speak in and of the archive. As you say, the archive is always already of the fathers or at best of the brothers, that is, defined by a cycle of parricide, therefore patriarchy.

But there is, as you might call it, a little *coup de théâtre* here, a dramatic twist to match Yerushalmi's. Last night, as I was making some checks of my referencing, I discovered an unexpected entry in the archive. Whether it was there before and I had not noticed, or has been changed since I last looked in the light of new information of which I am not aware, I do not know. But there it was. In the Screen Archive South East's database, the camera operator of several of the films shot in the 1940s, one of which contains the most erotic footage of the mystery woman as she bathes by a carp pond in her bikini, is listed not as 'TH Wistrand' as I had remembered but, to my surprise, as 'Mrs Wistrand or TH Wistrand', followed by a question mark.

In the footage the woman is radiant in a way that one can only be when gazed upon by a lover. This leads me to the question, might it not be Theodor Wistrand after all, but Catherine Wistrand who was the lover shooting the footage? This is an easy truth to make. Perhaps because I can't bear Theodor Wistrand possessing our shared love object, my mystery woman, or perhaps because it is true. Let's say that the mystery woman was the lover of Catherine Wistrand and it was she who recorded her in the Tokyo blossoms with her husband's camera. Theodor Wistrand either tolerated or turned a blind eye to his wife's lesbian relationship. Or perhaps he was gay himself and they had an arrangement, allowing him to comfortably film his wife and her lover in the deer park at Nara. Surely, if the mystery woman were the clandestine lover of Theodor Wistrand, her inclusion in the family scene would have made it appear awkward, but it doesn't. When the Wistrand's first met in Stockholm, perhaps it was not a whirlwind romance but a huge relief to find another queer person who wanted a marriage of convenience where each party could continue to see same-gender lovers. So Catherine's lover went with the family to Washington in 1939, while Theodor Wistrand went on his trip around Asia and was later stationed in Berlin. The war years spent frolicking by the coast were a happy time for Catherine and her lover. When her husband joined the family two years later, in 1941, Catherine borrowed his camera to film her lover by the water to keep the memory of her honey-warm caress forever close. Forgive me Professor, I drifted off and got excited. This story is not meant for you, though you may be interested as you said in your documentary, or rather the documentary on you (*Derrida* 2002), that you wanted to know more about people's sex lives, or at least about the sex lives of famous philosophers. Although I would like to know, this is not the question I have in mind for you.

You may think my mystery woman dreams and stories a soft deconstruction, but I do also have some more serious doubts about whether your final thesis is one to which I subscribe. I see at least three clues in your *Archive Fever* which suggest that the archive may be other than exclusively patriarchal or at best fraternal, as you claim it is. The first is your reading of the key thread linking Freud to Yerushalmi and by extension, Yerushalmi to yourself, and most significantly, the archive to the future, as an umbilical cord. Does the pertinent use of this distinctively female, nay matriarchal, metaphor on which your conceptualization of the archive is poised, not suggest that this institution harnesses a maternal rather than paternal power? Might the matriarchal quality of the archive be something that, superficially at least and, I expect with the goodwill of a self-defined feminist, you have unwittingly repressed?

The second clue is related to this. You use the noun *parricide* in French to refer to the killing of one's father, the Oedipal drive. The term *patricide* does not exist in French, though if it did I expect you would have used it, for it is clear that you want it to mean the killing of one's father specifically, rather than of any relative (as the word *parricide* technically can). The use of the word parricide is understandable, necessary even, in the French, but why allow this to be maintained in the English translation where, because we have the word *patricide*, parricide implies the killing of a close relative who is not necessarily the father. We have both committed parricide in this book, parricide of our mothers. To use your mother's term, as voiced by you in *Circumfession* (1993) when you write of her death, we are 'raising the stakes'. I say 'we' when speaking of your mother because, in what is at issue here, we—as children of dead mothers—have an equal stake.

To 'raise the stakes', your mother's term. Might the language of gambling which keeps cropping up in your work, particularly in these first, second, and third higher bids which conclude *Archive Fever*, be a hidden reference to the matriarch and the poker game of which she was so fond, and that she played even on the day of your birth? To be clear, I don't mean to say that you left the clues there on purpose, that you *planted* them, but that they are slips revealing something you have repressed. There is your mother, she is speaking through you, veiled under your writing on the 'patriarchal' archive. You can't help receiving her messages, Jackie. For Jackie is your real name given to you by your mother, after Jackie Coogan, a child-star of silent movies, a silent child through whom she perhaps hoped to speak.

But my question is not exclusively about mothers. I wish to ask of you whether the archive might be, or ever become, matriarchal. Let me put it another way: can a woman, a mother, a daughter, speak in and of the archive in her own name, can she make the truth? To re-appropriate Yerushalmi's umbilical cord opening of the future: much will depend, of course, on how the very terms *woman* and *truth* are to be defined. Right now, leaving the semantic and epistemological questions aside, I only want to know whether *you* ultimately came to believe it to be so. I will limit myself even further and be content if you answer only one question, phrased in Yerushalmi's terms: When Anna Freud conveyed those words to the congress in Jerusalem, *was she speaking in her own name?*

Please tell me, Professor, I promise I won't reveal your answer to anyone.

Works Cited:

Acker, Kathy (1978) *Kathy goes to Haiti* Rumour Publications Toronto
— (1993) *My Mother: Demonology, A Novel* Grove Press NY

Atwood, Margaret (1986) *The Handmaid's Tale* Verso

Bartlett, Thomas (2007) "Archive Fever" The Chronicle of Higher Education July 20, 2007

Blanchot, Maurice (1994/1998) *The Instant of my Death* translated by Elizabeth Rottenberg Stanford University Press Stanford and California

Carter, Angela (1978) "The Alchemy of the Word", in *Expletives Deleted: Selected Writings* London: Vintage 1992

Chang, Iris (1997) *The Rape of Nanking: The Forgotten Holocaust of World War II* Penguin

Darby Parry, Hamilton (1969) *The Panay Incident: Prelude to Pearl Harbor* Macmillan Toronto, NY

Deren, Maya (1985) *Divine Horsemen: The Living Gods of Haiti* McPherson & Co. US

Derrida, Jacques (1995) *Archive Fever: A Freudian Impression* University of Chicago Press, Chicago
— (1998) *Demeure: Fiction and Testimony* translated by

Elizabeth Rottenberg Stanford University Press Stanford and California
— with Bennington, Geoffrey (1993) *Jacques Derrida: Circumfession* The University of Chicago Press Chicago and London

Felman, Shoshana (1993) *What Does a Woman Want: Reading and Sexual Difference* Johns Hopkins University Press

Foucault, Michel (1972) *The Archeology of Knowledge and the Discourse on Language* Sheridan Smith, A (trans.) Pantheon Books, New York

Freeman, Derek (1983) *Margaret Mead and Samoa: the making and unmaking of an anthropological myth* Hammondsworth Penguin

Freeman, Derek (1998) *The Fateful Hoaxing of Margaret Mead: a historical analysis of her* Samoan Research Westview Press

Freud, Sigmund (1991, first published 1920) 'Beyond the Pleasure Principle' in *On Metapsychology: The Theory of Psychoanalysis vol.11* The Penguin Freud Library pp.275-305
— (1955 first Published 1919) 'The Uncanny' in *The Standard Edition of the Complete Psychological Works of Sigmund Freud* vol.17 Ed/trans. James Strachey London: Hogarth Press
— (1938[1934-38]/2001) *Moses and Monotheism: Three Essays* in The Standard Edition of the Complete Psychological Works of Sigmund Freud Volume XXIII Vintage

Fujioka, Nobukatsu and Jiyushungi Shikan Kenyukai, eds., (1996-98) *History not Taught in Textbooks 4 vols.* and *Shameful Modern History* Takuma Shoten Tokyo

Hu, Hua-Ling (2000) *American Goddess and the Rape of Nanking: The Courage of Minnie Vautrin* Southern Illinois University Press Carbondale and Edwardsville

Lévi-Strauss, Claude (1955/1973) *Tristes Tropiques* trans. John and Doreen Weightman, Cape: London

Mead, Margaret (1928) *Coming of age in Samoa: A Psychological Study of Primitive Youth for Western Civilization* Harper Collins
— (1942) *Balinese Character: A Photographic Analysis* University of California

Nozaki, Yoshiko (2005) "Japanese Politics and the History Textbook Controversy, 1945-2001 pp.275-306 in *History Education and National Identity in East Asia*, Vickers, E and Jones, A eds.). Routledge, New York

Ronell, Avital (1986) *Dictations: On Haunted Writing* University of Nebraska Press
— (1989) *The Telephone Book* University of Nebraska Press
— (2002) *Stupidity* University of Illinois Press
— (2005) *The Test Drive* University of Illinois Press Urbana and Chicago
— (2006) "Kathy Goes to Hell" in *Lust for Life: On the Writings of Kathy Acker* Scholder, Harryman, Ronell (eds.) Verso London

Spivak, Gayatri Chakravorty (1985) "The Rani of Simur: An essay on Reading the Archives' *History and Theory* 24,3 October
— (1999) *A Critique of Post-Colonial Reason* Harvard University Press, Cambridge Massachusetts

Sullivan, Patricia (2004) "*Rape of Nanking* Author Iris Chang Dies" *Washington Post* Friday, November 12, 2004:p B06

Yerushalmi, Yosef Hayim (1991) *Freud's Moses: Judaism Terminable and Interminable* Yale University Press

Works Consulted:

Amad, Paula (2010) *Counter-Archive: Film, the Everyday, and Albert Kahn's Archive de la Planète* Columbia University Press New York

Artaud, Antonin (1938/1958/1994) *The Theatre and its Double* Grove Press NY

Baker, Simon (2006) *Doctrines [The appearance of things]* Undercover Surrealism Ades, D and Baker, S (eds.) The MIT Press Cambridge and Massachusettes

Banner, Lois W. (2003) *Intertwined Lives: Margaret Mead, Ruth Benedict and their circle* Vintage New York

Bateson, G and Deren, M (1946/1980) 'An Exchange of Letters between Maya Deren and Gregory Bateson' *October* vol.14 (Autumn 1980) pp.16-20 MIT Press

Bateson, Mary Catherine (1984/2001) *With a Daughter's Eye: A Memoir of Margaret Mead and Gregory Bateson* Harper Collins, New York

Belo, Jane (1960) *Trance in Bali* Columbia University Press NY

Blake, Tara (2011) 'Planetary Counter-Archive' in New Formations, Issue.74
— with Harbord, Janet (2008) 'Typewriters, Cameras and Love Affairs: The Fateful Haunting of Margaret Mead'

Journal of Media Practice Vol.9, no.3 pp.215-227

Caffrey and Francis (2006) *To Cherish the Life of the World: Selected Letters of Margaret Mead* Basic Books

Clifford, James (1998) *The Predicament of Culture: Twentieth-Century Ethnography, Literature and Art* Harvard University Press, Cambridge Massachusetts

Clifford, James and Marcus, George E. (eds) (1986) *Writing Culture: The Poetics and Politics of Ethnography* University of California Press, Berkeley, Los Angeles, London

Derrida, Jacques (1967/1997) *Of Grammatology* trans. Gayatri Spivak The John Hopkins University Press: Baltimore and London
— (1987) *The Post Card* trans Alan Bass University of Chicago Press
— (1996) *The Gift of Death* trans. David Wills Chicago University Press

Heidegger, M (1927/1962) *Being and Time* trans Marquarrie and Robinson Oxford: Basil Blackwell

Hertzmann, L and Newbigin, J (2020) *Sexuality and Gender Now: Moving Beyond Heteronormativity* Routledge

Lapsley, Hilary (1999) *Margaret Mead and Ruth Benedict: The Kinship of Women* University of Massachusetts Press

Leiris, Michel (1934/1950) *L'Afrique Fantome* Gallimard Paris

Lusty, Natalya (2007) *Surrealism, Feminism, Psychoanalysis* Routledge London and New York

Mead, Margaret (1937-1939/1977) *Letters from the Field 1925-1975* Harper and Row, New York
— (1973) *Blackberry Winter: My Earlier Years* Angus and Robertson Ltd, London
— and Bateson, Gregory (1977/2002) 'On the Use of the Camera in Anthropology' in *The Anthropology of Media: A Reader* Askew and Wilks (eds) Blackwell Publishers pp.41-46

Riley, Denise (2012) *Time Lived, Without its Flow* Capsule Editions London

Rony, Fatimah Tobing (1996) *Third Eye: Race, Cinema and Ethnographic Spectacle* Duke University Press
— (2006) "The Photogenic Cannot be Tamed: Margaret Mead and Gregory Bateson's *Trance and dance in Bali*" *Discourse* 28 No.1 Winter 2006 pp.5-27

Royle, Nicholas (2003) *The Uncanny* Manchester University Press

Russell, Catherine (1999) *Experimental Ethnography: The Work of Art in the Age of Video* Duke University Press Durham and London

Savarese, Nicola and Fowler, Richard (2001) "Antonin Artaud Sees Balnese Theatre at the Paris Volonial Exposition" *TDR (1988-)* Vol.45 No.3 Autumn, 2001 pp.51-77

Schad, John (2007) *Someone Called Derrida: An Oxford Mystery* Sussex Academic Press

Shankman, Paul (2009) *Derek Freeman and Margaret Mead: What did he know and when did he know it? Pacific Studies* Vol.32 No2/3 June-Sept

Steedman, Carolyn (2000) *Dust: The Archive and Cultural History* Manchester University Press

Archive Fevers
By Tara Blake

First published in this edition by Boiler House Press, 2022
Part of UEA Publishing Project
Copyright © Tara Blake, 2022

The right of Tara Blake to be identified as the Author of this work has been asserted by them in accordance with the Copyright, Design & Patents Act, 1988.

Cover Design and Typesetting by Louise Aspinall
Typeset in Arnhem Pro & Courier New
Printed by Tallinn Book Printers
Distributed by NBN International

Editorial Coordination by James Hatton

Proofreading by Clare Kernie

This book is sold subject to the condition that it shall not, by way of trade or otherwise, be lent, resold, hired out, stored in a retrieval system, or otherwise circulated without the publisher's prior consent in any form of binding or cover other than that in which it is published and without a similar condition including this condition being imposed on the subsequent purchaser.

ISBN: 978-1-911343-77-6